THE SPIDER:
CITY OF WHISPERING DEATH

THE
MASTER OF MEN!
SPIDER®

CITY OF
WHISPERING DEATH

By Grant Stockbridge

POPULAR PUBLICATIONS • 2021

PUBLISHING HISTORY

"City of Whispering Death" originally appeared in the April 1938 (Vol. 14, No. 3) issue of *The Spider* magazine. Copyright 2021 by Argosy Communications, Inc. All rights reserved.

CHAPTER 1
THE WHISPERING DEATH

W HEN THE Whisper of Doom sounded, a traitor died—this was the word that sped along the Underworld grapevine. No man could say exactly what the message meant, nor tell the source of its warning. Yet they learned—and the city's millions heard of its terrible fulfillment. Afterward, New York trembled and was afraid.

In the wake of that awesome whisper, the rackets flourished; and the new city administration, fearless and honest though it was, was left shaken to its foundations, helpless.

It reached Richard Wentworth—that whisper along the grapevine—where he sat at dinner in the exclusive Voyagers' Club, and a bleak look crept into his gray-blue eyes. He gazed steadily upon his guest, the commissioner of police, Stanley Kirkpatrick.

"I think your stool pigeon—is it Whitey Morgan?—gave you straight information," Wentworth said quietly. *"The thing I have been warning you about has come."*

Kirkpatrick's compressed lips relaxed slightly. He knuckled his immaculate mustache. "You're always sniffing disaster, Dick," he protested benevolently. "This is just some silly attempt to close the mouths of the Underworld."

Wentworth leaned forward. "Because the hoodlums were driven from the polls, because, in spite of all criminal efforts, the

1

Death was everywhere when the

Whisper of Doom struck!

ballots were honestly counted and you have a good city administration at last, you think the Underworld is beaten." He was
vehement. "I tell you the most powerful and fearless district
attorney in the world can't convict criminals without witnesses
to testify against them!"

Kirkpatrick continued to smile, and Wentworth rose to his
feet. "If you'll excuse me, Kirk," he said quietly, "I'm going to
have special precautions taken to guard those witnesses you have

2

hidden in my home. And I'm going to see what else I can learn about this Whisper of Doom!"

Kirkpatrick slowly frowned. "My best officers are guarding those Hamilton girls," he said, "and your home is a fortress. What else possibly could be done?"

Wentworth shrugged and his stride quickened toward the foyer. He had phoned his home, then went out to his sleek Daimler before the marquee. His turbaned chauffeur stood at the open door, and there was eagerness in the man's dark Eastern eye, which held always a hint of the dog-like idolatry with which he regarded his master.

"Trouble, master?" The Hindu asked happily. He read the meaning of that long, clipped stride, that forward thrust of confident shoulders!

"Down Fifth Avenue, Ram Singh," Wentworth directed crisply. "Then... *east!*"

Ram Singh's white teeth glistened behind his thick beard. He *salaamed*, clapped the door shut and sprang to the wheel. That cabalistic command meant they were bound for the haunts of the Underworld—and warfare! Ram Singh, gallant warrior Sikh that he was, was eager for it, but Wentworth's frown was worried....

SWIFTLY, AS the Daimler gathered speed, Wentworth drew the curtains. He touched a secret button beneath the left half of the rear seat. The seat slid forward, revolving, and revealed, hidden in its back, a closely hung wardrobe and a make-up tray with a lighted mirror. Wentworth's lean, spatulate fingers moved deftly over the tray and, under his skilled touch, his face took on different lines.

The new administration, glorying in its really great triumph at the polls, might believe the Underworld would accept defeat and disintegrate, but already Wentworth had heard the rumblings of a defensive alliance. The Underworld had long ago learned that the best defense was to attack! Where the first blow now would fall, no man could say—not even Wentworth. But this Whisper of Doom pointed the course he must follow.

Wentworth peered into the mirror and the face that stared back was no longer the clean-lined, cultured countenance of Richard Wentworth, wealthy clubman and dilettante of the arts. It was hawkish, predatory, the mouth a lipless gash. It was a face that the world of criminals had learned to dread—and to hate—as they feared not all the combined minions of the law! For Wentworth had become that mysterious nemesis of the lawless called the Spider—the secret avenger who carried his own law in twin holsters under his arms, and from whose inexorable verdict there was no appeal!

Wentworth smiled slowly, and on that bitter face, the expression turned ominous. However, the avenger's garb was not for him—yet. Rapidly, he made a few further changes in his appearance. When, presently, the limousine briefly slowed amid black shadows, it was a curious figure that darted out to the cover of an alley—a man who moved with shuffling gait, whose eyes blinked weakly behind dark, hooded spectacles, and whose pendulous lips were more prone to tremble in fright than to tighten into the menace of the Spider. But this man had entry into the haunts of the Underworld where he was accepted as a small-time safecracker. Richard Wentworth, the Spider, had become Blinky McQuade.

At the door where he knocked, presently, with a curiously broken rhythm, he was admitted with a muttered recognition. Behind the dark lenses, Wentworth's eyes shuttled keenly over the faces of the criminals assembled in this Underworld hangout—Balmy's Bit House. No police ever entered that door, and within were men whom all the Underworld knew—by reputation at least.

All were artists of crime and violence who, if they but suspected the real identity of Blinky McQuade—or even discovered he was in disguise—would slaughter him on the spot!

Wentworth was hardened to the risk—but when he sat down it was at an unoccupied table. Here the grapevine was at its best; here he would catch the first... *whisper of doom!* Abruptly, he felt tension crawl along his nerves. In a corner across the dingy, dim room, he recognized a man who never before had been allowed within these sacrosanct precincts. It was the stool pigeon whom Commissioner Kirkpatrick had mentioned—Whitey Morgan! Traitor, his Underworld associates would call him, and the warning was, "When the Whisper of Doom sounds, a traitor dies!"

A whisper to his right startled Wentworth, but it was only a crook gossiping, "Casaroma ain't running none. Maybe Casaroma is this here now whisper guy."

Wentworth's eyes narrowed as he spotted the speaker. Billikin Schaeffer, a moon-faced killer, was a strong-arm man in Mike Casaroma's food rackets. His companion bore the killer mark, too.

"He's getting a bunch of the big shots together tonight," Schaeffer went on. "I hear Casaroma has got the lowdown on where they hid them Hamilton dames!"

WENTWORTH FELT his shoulder muscles knot slowly. Casaroma couldn't have discovered that the Hamilton girls

were hidden in his home! He *couldn't*—it was a secret known only to Wentworth, Kirkpatrick, and the district attorney himself! The guardian police never left the
building and the D.A., Thomas Louis, was as much beyond suspicion as Kirkpatrick himself. Yet, Casaroma would pay thousands of dollars to find Ada and Frances Hamilton. Their testimony could send the food racketeer up the river for years!

A whisper to the left pulled Wentworth's head stiffly about.

"A lot of stoolies is scared stiff about this whisper guy."

Wentworth swore under his breath. Already the Underworld was becoming intimidated. If this Whisper of Doom really killed a stool pigeon, not all District Attorney Louis' skill and honesty could force testimony from criminals! Whitey Morgan... Wentworth half-rose from his chair. There was an increasing certainty in his mind that trouble centered around Morgan—that he was doomed! If he could get the man clear....

Then came another *whisper*—and this one was different! Wentworth's heart beat heavily in his throat. Every sound in the room died out, broken off short as a cut string. The whisper sliced through the mutter of voices like a deadly knife, edged, sibilant, ominous:

"When the Whisper of Doom sounds, a traitor dies!... Stand up, Whitey Morgan!"

Too late now for Wentworth to get Whitey Morgan out— even if he dared to risk the valuable identity of Blinky McQuade. His eyes swept the room. He could not discover the whisper's source yet it sounded near and menacing. A scream whipped Wentworth's gaze back to Whitey Morgan.

The man was on his feet. He took a few stumbling steps toward the exit. Words tumbled incoherently from his lips, and men shrank away from him as from a leper. Across his screaming terror, the whisper struck again, laughing. The sound was taunting, fiendish. And Whitey Morgan screamed again—in awful pain!

Morgan stopped in his tracks, bent slowly forward. He stared down at his body, drew his clenched fists into his sides. His clothing gaped, sliced side to side as if by an incredibly keen knife, and the flesh… Morgan screamed again. He struggled to close that awful rip with clutching hands that were instantly crimson. He pitched forward on his face.

"A traitor dies! He was a stool pigeon for the police! Death to all who talk!"

Wentworth was on his feet, as was everyone else in the room, but still could find no trace of the man who whispered. There was not a single thing to indicate how Morgan had been disemboweled. No one had been anywhere near him. In the room's dead silence, Morgan's rattling breath, the convulsive drumming of his feet in his death spasm, grew terribly loud. Then the Whisper of Doom laughed again.

"The Hamilton girls are next! Death to all who talk!"

A shudder jerked at Wentworth's body. God! Such a death must not overtake those brave, lovely girls, whose only crime was that they had dared to tell the truth about a killer! His eyes shuttled behind Blinky McQuade's dark glasses. He dared not leave first lest the Underworld label him traitor. Yet he must warn the guards at his home. He no longer doubted. Casaroma—or this Whisper of Doom—knew the hiding place of the Hamilton girls!

When word of this killing, by a voice and a death-weapon that struck out of the nothingness, spread through the Underworld, no criminal would dare to talk. Once let the girls fall victim to the same fate, and the district attorney was beaten. For then no one in the entire city—even the victims of rackets— would dare to testify! He had to get out, at once....

Wentworth snatched off his hat, waved it in the air.

"Hooray!" he called feebly. "Hurrah for the Whisper of Doom!"

Men stared stupidly at him, still locked in the shock of that whispering menace and sudden death. Some one echoed his cry, and the tension was broken, as Wentworth had hoped. Everyone began to talk at once. Men flocked to the bar and others crouched inquisitively beside Morgan's body. Wentworth waited an interminable while before he slipped to the telephone and called his home. Relief flooded him at the strong, confident voice of his man, Jackson.

"All quiet, sir," Jackson reported. "The girls are asleep, with the police at their door."

A SMALL worry persisted in Wentworth's mind and he sent Jackson to make sure. Seconds dragged past and Jackson did not return. Wentworth's hand knotted about the phone until his arm ached. With a clenched fist, he beat softly on his thigh. Why didn't Jackson return? Wentworth twisted in the booth and peered out into the dark hallway behind him. Was he seeing things, or had the pale blur of a face faded out into the shadows there, watching him! Wentworth's hand crept to the heavy gun beneath his arm… and still Jackson did not return. Impatiently, he jiggled the receiver hook.

"You're still connected, sir," the operator singsonged.

And then, Jackson's voice came over the wire, but its confidence was gone and there was a strained and shaken thinness to it that stabbed Wentworth's heart.

"What is it?" he demanded harshly.

"Three police guards," Jackson said raspingly. "They're dead… sliced open with knives!"

"The girls!" Wentworth snapped.

"Frances Hamilton is here," Jackson went on. "She's asleep in her room, but Ada—"

"Quick, damn it!"

"She's gone, sir," Jackson stammered. "Just… vanished. I've got men searching the house, but there's no sign of where she went or… I was up there a half-hour ago, and everything was all right, and…."

"Report to the police!" Wentworth rasped. "Don't leave Francis Hamilton's side for a moment. Shoot at any sound, even a… a *whisper!*"

Wentworth slammed up the receiver, charged out of the booth—then remembered that he was Blinky McQuade and that some one had been watching. His shoulders cringed slowly,

10

and the scowl that went with his weak eyes came back to his forehead. He stared piercingly into the shadows. They were empty, and yet... he had seen a face. He slipped back into the saloon, mind whirling. Why had Ada Hamilton been taken away instead of killed? Was some worse fate in store for her? Casaroma... Wentworth's eyes flashed over the barroom to find Billikin Schaeffer. The man had mentioned that Casaroma had called a meeting of big shots—alibi, or alliance? He must know. There was Schaeffer now, moving toward the door!

With no further thought for the suspicion he might arouse, Wentworth shuffled rapidly after him. Schaeffer was not important enough to be included in Casaroma's conference. If he knew of it, it was because he had a job to do in that connection. By the heavens, when the Spider got hold of him, he would talk and talk fast, in spite of the Whisper of Doom! A girl's life—a city's very law enforcement—hung in the balance!

A half-block behind Schaeffer, Wentworth slipped out into the pitch-black alley. When he reached the corner, he turned abruptly and stared back into the gloom. He could see nothing but he thought he had heard the door close again... and he remembered that face in the shadows....

CHAPTER 2
CROSS-FIRE!

A T ANOTHER time, Wentworth would have set a trap to learn if he was followed. Caution, bred of long years of battle, dictated that. But now there was no time! He must not lose Schaeffer's trail! He must seize the first opportunity to corner the man and make him tell what he knew. One factor alone favored him. Schaeffer was moving directly toward the private garage nearby where Ram Singh would be waiting with the Daimler.

Wentworth shook his head, impatiently. If he carried Schaeffer into that garage, the moon-faced killer would have to die to preserve the secret. The Spider executed the death sentence without compunction where he had delivered judgment, but he was not a merciless killer. He did not slay for such trivial personal cause as that. There must be another way....

Schaeffer was still walking swiftly along when Wentworth reached the corner, around which was his garage. With the quickness of thought, Wentworth turned it and raced to the garage. As he bounded through the door, he was stripping off coat, hat and spectacles.

"Put these on," he snapped at Ram Singh. "Walk along the street. If you are followed, take the man prisoner—*alive!* Turn up your coat collar and keep your head down to hide that beard."

Ram Singh's white teeth flashed briefly behind his beard as he obeyed, without question—as always. Within less than twenty seconds, he was outside the garage. A brief smile twisted Wentworth's lips as he watched him go. For no other man on earth, would Ram Singh have shed that sacred turban! It was odd, too, to see those military shoulders attempt to assume a slouch. It wouldn't fool anyone in daylight, but in this darkness....

While Wentworth thought, he was busy. He could not use the Daimler on such business as he rode tonight, but there was another, shabby car parked beside it—and its motor was no less powerful. In an instant, he had sprung behind its wheel, the doors levered up automatically at the flash of his headlights and he rolled into the street to take up Schaeffer's trail. His keen eyes spotted Ram Singh shuffling along the street, but detected no shadower. Perhaps the whole thing was in his imagination. Perhaps....

Within a block, Wentworth picked up Schaeffer's trail and saw the man enter a parked car and drive off. It was the normal caution of the Underworld which dictated that no auto must be left near the criminal hideout and, for once, Wentworth was glad of the care taken. It had permitted him to get his own car. As he drove, his mind making swift plans, one hand was effecting changes in his disguise. The similarity between the Spider and Blinky McQuade was deliberate. It needed only the removal of the spectacles, of the rubber plates that made his lips pendulous, a lank black wig drawn snugly over his head—and now it was the Spider who trailed Schaeffer. A slight, cold smile played upon the lipless gash that was his mouth. He had made his plans!

As the coupé ahead turned into a dark side street, Wentworth stepped on the gas and, an instant later, crowded Schaeffer to the curb—then called out in a sibilant whisper.

"When the Whisper of Doom sounds, wise men listen!" said Wentworth.

Through the windshield, he could see the white blur of Schaeffer's face. Wentworth's hand rested on his gun, but he must not kill. Schaeffer must live to talk!

Schaeffer's voice answered him, blurred and frightened "I ain't done nothing!" he called frantically. "I swear I ain't, Whisper!"

"Get in my car!" Wentworth ordered, still whispering. *"I know the right men, too!"*

Schaeffer was climbing out of his car in terrified eagerness, hurrying toward him. Once more the cold smile of the Spider touched Wentworth's lips. It was going to be easy after all. He

"This man has talked. When the Whisper of Doom sounds—a traitor dies!"

would pose as the Whisper and worm the information he sought from Schaeffer, then to the conference of the big shots, and....

The pistol shot came from some distance away. The sound of the bullet punching through the back window, within inches of Wentworth's head, seemed to come ahead of it. Then a man's voice, shrill and penetrating, ran along the street.

"That's not the Whisper, Schaeffer. *Kill him!*"

SCHAEFFER WAS within a yard of Wentworth's coupé, but at the cry, he hurled himself backward to the shelter of his own car and a gun leaped to his fist. Wentworth swore and batted open the door of the car, farthest from Schaeffer. As he flung to the street, sprawling his length on the pavement, the gun behind hammered again. But his own car was no protection. He was caught in the deadly cross-fire that the Underworld murderers had perfected—from behind and from the side. He could still probably reach and kill Schaeffer, but he wanted the man alive... and the second gunman was crouched behind a parked car a full fifty feet away!

Lead hammered the metal back of the car, gashed the asphalt beside the Spider. With a lunge, he rolled beneath his machine toward Schaeffer. If he could disarm the man... His twin .45 caliber automatics were heavy in his hands. He paused for an instant, hammered out four swift shots along the surface of the street toward the parked car behind which the unseen gunman lurked—then elevated his weapons and threw two more through the body of the car itself. From the corner of his eye, he caught a glint of gun metal. Schaeffer was thrusting his weapon around the hood of the engine at point-blank range!

With a frantic roll, Wentworth brought a gun to bear and squeezed the trigger in the same instant. He heard his lead strike tinnily on the car's hood, heard a man scream! Damn it, if he had killed Schaeffer... The understructure of the car had cramped his arm, hampered his aim. Twice more, he fired toward the parked car, the noise of his shots thunderous in his ears. The empty street rolled with the echoes, but there was no answer. Cautiously, Wentworth eased out from beneath the car on the side nearest Schaeffer. His ears were ringing with concussion. He closed his nostrils, blew hard to equalize the pressure, and began to hear again. He heard the hoarse breathing of a dying man!

A bitter curse leaped to Wentworth's lips. He darted around the car. Schaeffer lay, spread out limply, on the sidewalk. From beneath him spread a dark stain. God, he must work fast! The Spider's mouth drew into a bitter, hard line. He doubled forward, guns clenched and ready, and raced toward the parked car. His feet beat slapping echoes from the pavement; his breath came sharp and thin between his teeth. There was no other sound. He sprinted past the parked car, gun swiveling to throw lead— and found there was *nothing* there. Nothing behind the car, nor inside of it. The other gunman had fled!

With a worried frown, Wentworth stared keenly about the street. But Schaeffer was dying, and before death sealed his lips, he must talk! Wentworth raced back to the wounded gunman, knelt beside him. He poured whisky from a pocket flask he always carried, between the man's lips, and presently Schaeffer's eyes opened heavily. At sight of the menacing face of the Spider so close, his eyes flew wide and a shudder ran through him.

"I want one thing from you," Wentworth said raspingly. "Talk, and I'll take you to a hospital. Refuse, and—" he lifted his heavy automatic where the man could see it—"a slug from this goes through your belly!"

Schaeffer gasped hoarsely, blood wetting his lips. "Don't... don't shoot!" he whispered.

Wentworth's lips were thin. He didn't like this bullying of dying men, but he knew that Schaeffer had killed... and his kind laughed when their victims died!

"Where is Casaroma holding his conference?"

He pointed the big mouth of the automatic downward, and Schaeffer quivered. "Don't!" he gasped. "Don't... It's in the penthouse, but for God's sake..." He shuddered, his body jerked and he twisted violently on his side while blood gushed from his lips. As Wentworth straightened, death stopped the man's spasms.

Wentworth stood, staring grimly down at the man. It was justice that had been done here—the Spider's justice. Wentworth's hand moved to his vest pocket and slipped out a platinum cigarette lighter. In an instant, he had thumbed open the base and pressed it against the dead gangster's forehead. Moments later, Wentworth was back in his own car, speeding through the dark streets, but he had left behind a warning that the Spider once more had taken the trail against crime—against the Whisper of Doom! For on Schaeffer's chilling flesh, he had left a crimson-gleaming symbol, a figure of sprawling hairy legs and poison fangs—*the seal of the Spider!*

Fortunately, he knew the location of Casaroma's penthouse, as the Spider made it his business to know the head-quarters of all important criminals in the city. It was twenty stories above Central Park West, on the roof of an  exclusive apartment building, which, rumor said, Casaroma owned. It would not be easy to reach, but the Spider had in the holsters beneath his arms the keys to even stronger fortresses! However, it must be done without raising an alarm.

WENTWORTH PARKED the car and slid into the dark trade entrance of the building Casaroma was supposed to own. It was strongly barred with steel, but there was a lock and Went-worth quickly unfastened it with a lock-pick of surgical steel. It was a long climb up the fire stairs, but his progress was unim-peded. It was as if Casaroma knew no one who dared enter his modern fortress could possibly escape.

Wentworth smiled slightly, the movements of his lips compressed, stern. If he found here what he expected, there would be many who would not escape alive! No doubt that Casaroma at least knew of Ada Hamilton's disappearance, and where to find her. No one else could be interested in her disappearance. It was strange that the other girl had not been harmed....

Wentworth finally reached the roof level and made a cautious reconnaissance. By mounting the elevator shaft to the machin-ery room, he would reach the roof of Casaroma's penthouse. He used the emergency lock on the shaft doors, applying his steel pick once more, and with twenty stories of emptiness beneath him, peered upward to the machinery. The cable drum was supported on two parallel steel beams. Hurriedly, Wentworth drew out a slender length of rope that always accompanied the Spider's expeditions. It was woven of silk and, while only the thickness of a pencil in diameter, yet would support seven hundred pounds weight with its elastic strength!

In a matter of seconds, he looped the silken rope over the beams above and, supporting himself by the strands which the police knew as the Spider's web, closed the door behind him. It wasn't easy to climb that slender line, but by twisting it alternately about his arms, Wentworth went upward, hand over hand. The wind that swept the roof was soft with summer, strangely in contrast with the grim death that threatened. Wentworth bowed his head to it as his eyes quested about. Instantly, his gaze fell upon a skylight and he reached it with long bounds, peered cautiously downward into Casaroma's apartment.

The room below him was fitted out with all the formal magnificence of the directors' conference chamber in some huge corporation. Even as Wentworth stared, men were filing into that room—men the Spider knew and detested. A meeting of big shots, Schaeffer had called it, and truly these men were five kings of crime. Mike Casaroma, with a treacherous smile on his swarthy face, had the food rackets in thrall. There was the lean, cadaverous Horton Kingsley to whom District Attorney Louis had been trying to pin responsibility for the restaurant troubles. Beside him, the squat, blunt-featured Chopper Gow, who ruled the labor rackets, looked like a savage. But Wentworth knew that of the two, Kingsley was the more deadly! The other men, Black Bloxton and Dutch Gordon split the gambling proceeds of the city. If these five, and their mobs, were going to work together, it was time that the Spider entered the lists! He could catch the mumble of their voices now, but no words.

Wentworth searched for some means of opening the skylight, but it was screwed down tightly all around. Perhaps, if only one would speak at a time... He leaned forward in an attempt to read their lips.

Casaroma was laughing. "What would I know about the Whisper..." Wentworth caught that much before the head turned away. The Spider's hand crept to his gun. What a favor he would confer upon the world if he rid it of these parasites! Slowly, Wentworth shook his head. He was no assassin to strike from the dark, even against wolves such as these. He could smash the skylight and leap down among them. But what guarantee did he have that, among these men, he would strike down this new power which called itself the Whisper of Doom? His methods were not those of these gangsters. The death of these kings would mean only that their lieutenants would seize the reins, and the Whisper....

ABRUPTLY, WENTWORTH grew rigid and a startled oath escaped from between his grim lips. For the double-doors at the end of the room had flung open and an incredible, nightmare figure stood confronting the five gangsters! The man—if indeed it was a man—was clad from shoulders to toes in a long, trailing robe of purple silk. That part of the body was human enough, but the head was that of a demon! The features were gargoyle and horrible, the eyes twisted into leering slits, the mouth a cruel gash! Then the figure stepped into better light, and Wentworth saw that the head was a mask—such as Eastern priests wear in fantastic rituals of sacrifice!

Slowly, Wentworth drew his automatic. A suspicion had leaped to his mind that this time he had found… the Whisper! He stared at the gangsters. Mocking grins were on the faces of most of them, but there was bewilderment, too. Then Wentworth heard the whisper that had reached through the saloon to herald Whitey Morgan's death. Through some trick of phonetics, it penetrated where the deeper, blurred tones of the men had not.

"Casaroma," it said, *"I promised you certain things—as proof that I can do what I claim. I promised to deliver a traitor.…"*

He paused and, through the door from behind him, a man hurtled as if expelled from a gun. He sprang to his feet and cringed against the wall, eyes wide, lips slavering with terror.

"This man has talked to the police! When the Whisper of Doom sounds, a traitor dies!"

As he spoke, the man against the wall screamed and, as with Whitey Morgan, his body was suddenly ripped open from side to side! Wentworth thought he caught the glitter of some flying weapon, but it happened too quickly for him to see and, certainly, there was no trace of it afterward. The man was writhing on the floor, and the smiles were gone from the faces of the five kings of crime. Chopper Gow had drawn a gun, and the whisper sliced through the dying screams of the man on the floor.

"Put that gun away, Gow, or do you want to die as he did?"

22

Gow stared down at the man and, brutal primitive though he was, he shuddered and slowly put away the gun. Casaroma took three slow steps forward, and his raised voice penetrated dimly to Wentworth's ears.

"All right now," Casaroma said thickly. "Let's have the second part of your promise, Whisper. The Hamilton girls—I know one of them's been snatched! It's on the police radio."

Wentworth's lips twisted harshly. He leveled his automatic at the Whisper's throat. That mask might be of steel and the man's body might be similarly protected under that robe, but the throat…. A curse leaped to his lips. A girl, clad only in a flimsy nightdress, catapulted through the door as the man had done, and he recognized the dark loveliness of Ada Hamilton! Wentworth's hand tightened on the butt of his automatic, but, even as he was squeezing the trigger, he heard a step behind him on the roof!

Wentworth's turn was liquid lightning for speed, but even so he could not entirely dodge the attack. A man was crouched over him and the light from the skylight glittered on the weapon in his hand. It was a hatchet, razor sharp. It sliced straight down at Wentworth's head!

CHAPTER 3
DEATH ON THE ROOF!

EVEN A shot could not stop the swift descent of that blade in time to save Wentworth's life. Besides, he dared not fire. The sound would bring the entire armed force of Mike

Casaroma down upon him, doom him more surely than this murderous hatchet.

What Wentworth did was purely reflex—the result of the months and years of warfare that lay behind him. As he rolled, he lashed out with his legs. His knees struck against the killer's ankles and threw him off-balance. The blade hissed down. Wentworth felt it jar against his head, the rasp of its metal on the gravel roof. Pain blinded him, and a mad desire for laughter pumped in his throat. What had saved him was the Spider's wig upon his head! Its thickness had misled his assailant and the hatchet had sliced through it, barely grazing Wentworth's scalp.

While that thought flickered through Wentworth's brain, he was fighting. With the blow, the assassin had pitched forward across Wentworth's body. The Spider flung frantic arms about him, but failed to pinion the man. Muscles leaped out like steel cables across the assassin's shoulders as he fought to lift the hatchet again. Wentworth was forced to drop the gun. His hands slid, lightning swift, up over the man's shoulders and under his chin in a reverse double Nelson. It was a deadly hold. He could drive the other's head back between his shoulders, snap his spine—if the hatchet did not sink first into his own skull!

Explosively, Wentworth threw all his strength and will into straightening his crooked arms, into forcing the man's head up and back. He could feel the writhing strength of those shoulders. He heard the hatchet rasp as it was lifted up from the roof. A single blow from that would finish the fight. Wentworth's eyes were strained wide, staring upward at the man with whom he fought. He was conscious, strangely, of the bite of the rough gravel against the back of his neck, the chill brush of the wind across the roof. Dimly, he could hear the voice of the Whisper, but his own breath was hoarse and rasping in his throat—like the panting respirations of the man he fought.

Wentworth's legs stiffened, back arching with the fury of his effort. His arms were numbing with the effort, wrists aching with the upward strain. And still that hatchet lifted, slowly, methodically, as if the man knew that this one stroke must do the trick. He would not be able to see where to strike, but he would not need to. A single, chopping gash with that edge beneath him... *The blow started down!*

Wentworth's eyes flew wide at the downward sweep on that deadly weapon. His arms already were exerting their utmost strength but, against the bull power of those muscle-knotted shoulders, it was not enough. Not enough... Wentworth did the only thing left to him. As that blade slashed down, he dug his right foot desperately against the roof and rolled. Once more, the hatchet grated on the gravel, but Wentworth's strength was waning. He knew now that he could not prevail with this hold. With the roll, he released his grip, drove his knees upward into the man's body and reeled to his feet. He was barely in time. Bent forward from the pain of Wentworth's blow, the man was lurching toward him, with the hatchet raised!

Desperation raced through Wentworth. If he had had his gun, he would have fired, but it lay somewhere in the darkness upon the roof. Death was very close, and it was not only his own life that was at stake, but the life of that helpless girl below—and the involved fate of the city. Wentworth pulled his head down and leaped to the attack! A scant yard away from the man, he checked and wavered back. The hatchet slashed past him so close that it gashed the lapel of his coat!

Instantly, Wentworth sprang in. He shuttled past the man and, as he leaped by, his hooked elbow caught beneath the killer's chin. All his weight and the power of his leap went into that head-lock, and he bent sharply forward at the waist. He spilled to his knees with the suddenness of his stop, but the weight of the assassin was gone from his shoulders. He jerked up his head, saw the hurtling black shape pin-wheeling through the air toward the brick balustrade that surrounded the roof.

Wentworth thrust himself to his feet, as the man struck. He went reeling forward. His arms hung limply at his sides, his head sagged... but he went forward. The man lay in a formless huddle against the balustrade, and Wentworth stared at the up-turned face with a sense of growing bewilderment. A Chinese hatchet man!

Wentworth twisted about to the lighted skylight and ran, staggeringly, toward it. His eyes quested frantically about for his guns. Damn it, he should have known! Such methods as that whispering death could come only out of the horror chambers of the East. America's Underworld was bad enough, God knew, but if with it was to be combined the infamy of the Orient, then Heaven help the city! That man in his purple silken robes and demon's mask... With a gasp of triumph, Wentworth spotted his gun. He snatched it up, sprang to the skylight and saw… *nothing.* The conference room was empty!

WENTWORTH DARTED across the roof toward the side that gave on Casaroma's terrace, stared down. It was deserted and there was no gleam of light from within. In three bounds, he was across and peering down at the street twenty stories below. Two long, sleek cars stood there and, even from this distance, he could distinguish the squat figure of Chopper Gow, the lank gauntness of Horton Kingsley. They were going, damn them, and Ada Hamilton probably was in one of those cars. By the time he could reach them….

Fury twisted the Spider's face. With long strides, he crossed to the Chinese he had killed. An instant sufficed to print on his forehead the seal of the Spider. Then he heaved up the body and ran, staggering to the railing. For an instant, he poised it there, then hurled it out into space! If only it would delay them for a few moments! Wentworth did not wait to see the body strike. He whirled and hand-vaulted the railing to the terrace below. He fell, sprawling, was up instantly and racing toward Casaroma's apartment. The French doors crashed inward under the impact of his shoulder. A frightened man-servant stared at him. Wentworth was beside him in an instant, face grim.

"That girl!" he demanded. "Where did they take her?"

The man trembled under his piercing eyes. "That man in purple," he stammered. "The Whisper? He went out with her!"

"Where did they go?"

"I don't know, sir. I swear to God, I don't know!" The man

dropped on his knees. "He wouldn't tell the boss. Said he'd take care of her!"

A groan of despair welled out of Wentworth's throat. The Chinese had a way of "taking care" of their victims! Casaroma didn't know—or pretended not to know—who this Whisper was. He'd wring the truth out of the big shot! Long bounds carried him to the door. Wentworth stood quivering with impatience while the private elevator shot upward to answer his ring. He sprang inside, and one of Casaroma's men stared at him, snatched at a gun. Wentworth's fist found his jaw and he threw the lever himself, sent the cage shooting downward. They would be lying in ambush for him downstairs. Wentworth whipped out his automatic and weighed it on his palm. Bitter laughter beat from his lips. A girl's life was at stake!

As the elevator neared the first floor, Wentworth set his thigh against the lever and bent over the gunman on the floor, hauled him up as a shield before him. He released the lever then, wrenched open the door and sprang out.

A uniformed hall boy stared at him with a gaping mouth. There was no one else in sight! Wentworth hurled the unconscious guard from him, punched open the front doors, and raced for the corner. Around there had stood the cars toward which he had hurled the Chinese's body. He sprang wide of the corner, guns ready in his fists. On the sidewalk lay the crushed body of the hatchet man, and beneath him, lay another. His pale, dead face was that of one of Casaroma's bodyguards. The cars had vanished!

Wentworth swore fiercely and, in the distance, police sirens made a thin whining like a cold winter wind. They must not find the Spider here! For all of Richard Wentworth's friendship with Stanley Kirkpatrick, their commissioner, there was only deadly enmity for the Spider among the police. In their eyes he was a criminal and his executions of the guilty were murder.

Wentworth ran swiftly. His fleeing figure blended with the shadows and, moments later, his shabby coupé was speeding through the city streets. His mind was working furiously. Before it was too late to save Ada Hamilton, he must trace down the men who had kidnaped her. If he demanded it, Kirkpatrick would probably put out a general alarm for Casaroma, but the police would not be able to make him talk. There was always the chance that he spoke the truth—that he did not know the Whisper nor what had been done with the girl. Precious time would be lost—minutes that might mean life or death to Ada Hamilton.

Only one other way. Wentworth must discover how the information as to her whereabouts had leaked out, tear the truth from whomever had talked. It could not be anyone in his own household, and he knew Kirkpatrick had trusted no one with the facts. But District Attorney Louis, for all of his success, was fairly new to criminal ways. He might have trusted some one, and been betrayed. He would not yet know the power of criminal gold.

For brief minutes, Wentworth parked in a dark side street, repairing the damage of the battle. Then, with hat drawn low over his eyes, he slid into a drugstore telephone booth, called the district attorney's office. It was well after midnight, but with the hunt on for Ada Hamilton, Louis would probably be there. Wentworth's guess was right.

"Richard Wentworth speaking," he said in his normal quiet tones. "Put me through to Mr. Louis at once."

His name opened the wires to him, and the crisp, disturbed tones of the district attorney came to him swiftly.

"Louis," Wentworth clipped out, "what I am going to say reflects no discredit upon you or your office, but I want to know the names of everyone connected with you who knew Ada Hamilton was at my home."

"No one," Louis said strenuously. "Absolutely no one except myself and a man who has been with me through all my investigations—my own brother!"

"Delehanty?" Wentworth said slowly.

"Exactly!"

"You've talked with him?" Wentworth asked then. "Is he there now?"

Louis' voice rose harshly with indignation. "Yes, I questioned him," he said, "and he has told no one—no one at all. It may interest you to know that Commissioner Kirkpatrick is satisfied! We let him go home!"

LOUIS SLAMMED up the receiver, and Wentworth wheeled out of the booth, once more sent his car racing through the streets. Kirkpatrick might be satisfied. Richard Wentworth should be, since he knew Delehanty Louis for a man of impregnable honesty—his reputation scarcely less than that of his elected brother. Yet—the Whisper had found Ada Hamilton.

It was a mad risk he intended to run, but the Spider was going to call on the district attorney's brother! He had been forced to use his real name in order to get the information from Louis; but only the Spider could extract hidden facts from Delehanty Louis—if there were any to learn! He would run greater risks than that to save Ada Hamilton and avert the blow which her death would strike at all law enforcement.

Once more, the Spider crept in through a dark trade entrance and raced upward unseen by deserted stairways. At the door of Delehanty Louis' apartment, he paused only long enough to use the lock-pick, then he was inside. He listened intently, peered about.

A dim night-light burned in the hall, but at its far end a door stood open and there was more illumination there. As Wentworth peered, a man's pacing figure moved across the oblong of light, vanished for a long moment, then returned. Delehanty Louis, hands knotted behind his sturdy back, was pacing the floor of his study—his face that of a tortured man!

Silent as the creature whose name he bore, Wentworth crept along that dim hallway and reached the side of the study door, unobserved. He peered into the room. Before a mirror which hung low on the wall, stood the prosecutor's brother. His lips were grimly locked and, as Wentworth stared, the lines of torture were slowly erased. His shoulders came back and his firm mouth twisted into a smile. Words came from him in a blurred murmur and Wentworth strained his ears.

"As long as you keep your mouth shut!" said Delehanty Louis.

Wentworth's eyes turned cold as glacial ice. There was no doubt in his mind now. Delehanty Louis had sold out his brother and, because of that, a girl would die, and a suffering city.... The Spider went into the room. In two strides, his hand closed on the man's shoulder, and the violence of the attack sent Louis reeling backward half across the study and into a deep leather chair. Louis stared, his face gray and frightened, his long jaw lax.

"But you're not going to keep your mouth shut, Louis," the Spider said flatly. "You're going to talk, fast and straight, or...." Wentworth's left hand scooped the cigarette lighter out of his pocket and, with a swift movement, he jammed its base on the back of Louis' hand. Louis gasped, snatched his hand away and then stared with terror-stricken eyes at the red seal that glistened on its back—*the seal of the Spider!* Fumblingly, he rubbed it with his palm in an effort to get it off.

"It will never come off, Louis," Wentworth said flatly. "That's for the hand that took filthy Judas money to betray an innocent girl!"

"No!" Louis gasped. "No, as God is my witness, I didn't!"

"Talk," the Spider ordered. "Tell me whom you told about Ada Hamilton—or that seal will be drawn on your forehead, *in your own blood!*"

Delehanty Louis started to his feet, but the bitter eyes of the Spider rested on his, and drove him back. He leaned forward, talking excitedly.

"I swear I didn't sell her out!" he cried. "It was blackmail! I had either to tell that or destroy my own brother. I had to talk! And afterward I tried to get Tom to move her somewhere else. I swear to you I did!"

The man's tone carried the note of desperation, almost of

truth. Wentworth stared at him. He reached up slowly to the gun beneath his arm, snaked it into view. He laughed, the sound mocking, flat, threatening.

"Whom did you tell?" he demanded again. He saw Louis had a gun, too.

Louis sank back in the chair. "I can't tell," he whispered. "If I do, hell… he'll ruin Tom! I tell you…" His hands sank to his thighs, his head bowed. "Go ahead and shoot me. I won't tell."

Wentworth stood there, frowning. He knew that he would not kill Louis for keeping his secret. Murder was not the Spider's forte. On the other hand, he *must* learn the name of….

Then he had time for no further speculation, for the window drapes abruptly rustled, from out their depths a fisted gun thrust—and the room shook with its explosion. Too late, Wentworth sprang for that assassin. The man was gone!

Wentworth saw what had happened, even before his shoulders touched the wall toward which he had hurled himself. The shock of that sight pinned him there against the wall, motionless, without strength. He had no need to look at Louis, twisted grotesquely sidewise across the arm of his chair where the heavy beat of the lead had hurled him. He was already dead. Even as Wentworth stared, the inertia of death loosened his muscles and Louis spilled to the floor, flat on his back. His right hand lay across his chest and on it shone the seal of the Spider!

Behind Wentworth, a quavering voice spoke. "Stand just like that, or, as God is my witness, I'll shoot you down!"

Wentworth twisted about to stare into the wide blue gaze of

a girl. In her trembling hand was an automatic pistol, and her twitching finger already was tight upon the trigger!

CHAPTER 4
DEATH TO THE SPIDER!

STRANGELY, IT was pity rather than fear which stirred the heart of the Spider, though he realized fully the peril of his position. That gun was far more dangerous in this nervous girl's hand than the most experienced of Mike Casaroma's torpedoes. This poor girl… and her brother lying dead on the floor. He pitied her, yet could not pause. Another such girl as herself equally deserving of his help, was in the hands of the Whisper.

Wentworth's hands lifted, and he stepped slowly aside. The girl's wide, frightened eyes jerked from him to the interior of the study. Her lips flew wide in a scream and, with a quick step, Wentworth had the gun.

"I'm sorry for you," he said quietly. "Believe me, the death of your brother was not my doing. A man out there…" His protest died—where was his evidence of innocence?

If the girl heard him, she paid no heed. She scarcely seemed aware that he had plucked the gun from her hand. She stared, then her pale face turned up to him.

"The Spider," she whispered. "The Spider! But why? Dely never did any one any harm, and you…" Her voice broke and she hurled herself upon him, tearing at his face with her nails, beating at his chest with small white fists.

Sick at heart, Wentworth turned away from her and fled. Her

screams pursued him. She ran to the door, shrieking, and people popped out of their apartments. A man fired wildly, and the crash of the shot echoed endlessly through the halls. Wentworth streaked down the steps and his face was very grave.

Delehanty Louis undoubtedly deserved death, but this was going to be damnably serious to the Spider. Richard Wentworth had called the district attorney to discover who had known of Ada Hamilton's hideout. The Spider would be accused of killing the brother. There was the seal on his hand to prove it. Probably, Wentworth and Kirkpatrick were the only persons who knew that the brother had been told.

To make matters even more serious, Commissioner Kirkpatrick had long been convinced that Wentworth and the Spider were one. He had never found the proof, but he had served warning on Wentworth that if he ever did he would prosecute to the full limit of the law. His stern regard for duty would permit no less than that. What would happen now, Wentworth could only guess... and worse still his course lay now directly to police headquarters. It seemed to him that Kirkpatrick could do no less than pick up Casaroma and, through the racketeer, lay Wentworth's only clue to the whereabouts of Ada Hamilton.

Back in his car, Wentworth raced toward his near-by home behind Sutton Place—the mansion that was a veritable fortress built behind sturdily defended walls on filled-in land between two piers. He slammed the car into the private garage on one of the short dead-end streets east of Sutton Place, raced through an underground corridor. He must change to his own identity... As he hurried into a secret dressing-room, he jabbed a wall button and, moments later, Ram Singh hurried into the room.

"The man that was following you," Wentworth snapped at him. "What happened to him?"

Ram Singh lifted his cupped hands in *salaam*. "No man followed me, *sahib*," he said regretfully. "It was perhaps that my disguise was not successful."

Wentworth swore under his breath as the ointments took off the Spider's makeup. Of course, what Ram Singh said was accurate. The battle on the roof of Casaroma's penthouse proved that. It was plain that the racketeer's men had known nothing of it. The Chinese had been a henchman of the Whisper!

"The *missie sahib* is upstairs, *sahib*," Ram Singh said. "She came after word of the kidnaping was given out. She wishes to see you before you go."

Wentworth's lips softened, as he peered at his reflection in the mirror, inspecting it to make sure the last traces of make-up were gone. Nita van Sloan was the only woman in the world who knew the secret of his double identity. More than once, she had joined him in his deadly battles—had gone in imminent peril of her life. But she must not be endangered this time—the situation was too serious!

"I'll be up in two minutes," he told Ram Singh quietly, sprang to a closet and began to pull on a fresh suit. The Sikh *salaamed* and left and, presently, Wentworth followed him. Nita was waiting quietly for him in the drawing-room on the top floor. SHE ROSE with an eager smile, her outstretched hands greeting him. Wentworth folded her in his arms. It had been no longer than afternoon since he had seen her, but for them each fresh meeting must always take on the nature of thanksgiving, such was the peril in which the Spider moved.

He held her off, gazed deeply into her violet eyes. Abruptly then, he was no longer the lover, but the man of action. Swiftly, he outlined to her the happenings of the night and, as he spoke, Nita's face grew grave.

"They'll arrest you for Louis' death," she said with a catch in her throat. "There's no way to avoid it."

Wentworth agreed with a nod. "You must be ready to get my lawyers down to headquarters. A writ. Damnable to use those gangster tactics, but I must not remain in prison now—too much depends on my liberty. And I've got to go to headquarters at once, or that poor girl... Kirkpatrick has picked up Casaroma, hasn't he? Good! Have you any idea of what happened here?"

Nita shook her head. "All that I can find out is that an extra policeman came in this evening, apparently with a message from Kirkpatrick, and remained. He must have let the kidnapers in. I can't get any adequate description of him."

Wentworth's lips closed in an angry line. So it had been as simple as that, and three policemen had died. Ada....

"I'm on my way," he said shortly. "Darling, I need you to stay in this house and see that nothing else of the kind happens to Frances Hamilton. I have no time to talk with her now."

He clasped Nita briefly to him again and was gone, this time with Ram Singh at the wheel of his Daimler. Minutes dragged out into seeming hours while he sped down the east side and turned toward Centre Street.

"If I'm taken out of here by policemen," he directed the Sikh shortly, "you are to follow until you find where I am taken, then call Miss Nita and report. I'm expecting to be arrested."

"*Wah, sahib!*" Ram Singh cried. "No need to call the *missie sahib!* With my knives…."

"We do not fight the police, Ram Singh," Wentworth said quietly. "You have your orders."

"Thy servant hears and obeys," Ram Singh said.

Wentworth leaned back against the cushions and closed his eyes. Behind lowered lids, his mind was racing. It was madness to go thus to headquarters and risk the inevitable delay, and yet what other course was open to him? Wait until Casaroma was released, then seize him? But that would be a task for an army under the guns of his bodyguards. No, no, there was no other way.

Wentworth walked calmly up the steps of headquarters and the green lights threw a sickly glow over his chiseled features. The man in the information booth stared at him, started to call out—and pressed a button beneath his desk. Wentworth saw

RICHARD WENTWORTH

all those things, under cover of his quiet nod of greeting to the man, and knew that orders for his arrest already had gone out. He moved deliberately up the stairs.

"Announce me to the commissioner, please," he threw at the man in the booth.

The die was certainly cast now—past all recall....

39

AS WENTWORTH turned into the outer office, the door of Kirkpatrick's private quarters flung open, and the militant figure of the commissioner filled the lighted oblong. He said nothing, but his face was stern and angrily flushed as Wentworth greeted him gravely and walked past. District Attorney Louis glowered at him.

"Where's Casaroma?" Wentworth asked shortly. "I have reason to know he has seen Ada Hamilton tonight. We've got to make him talk."

Kirkpatrick had pivoted at the doorway, but gave no other sign that he knew of his existence. Louis' face was haggard.

"Wentworth," he said heavily, "you called tonight and asked me who knew of the girl's hideout in your home."

Wentworth agreed with a quiet nod. "You said Kirkpatrick was satisfied of his innocence. That's enough for me."

Kirkpatrick's voice rasped in his throat. "It wasn't enough for the Spider!"

Wentworth spun toward him, his face frowning, puzzled. "For the Spider!" he exclaimed. "What do you mean?"

Kirkpatrick's face lost its anger, became weary and Wentworth's heart was suddenly filled with misery. This was the moment he had dreaded more than any other in his long life of Underworld battles. Both men had seen that it was inevitable, and each knew what Kirkpatrick's course must be. Kirkpatrick braced his shoulders.

"Wentworth," he said flatly, "I'm arresting you for the murder of Delehanty Louis tonight at his apartment!"

Louis uttered a gasp of amazement, took a sharp, chopping

stride forward. "Do you mean. Kirkpatrick, that this man… that Richard Wentworth…."

Kirkpatrick said heavily, "I've believed that Wentworth and the Spider were one, for many months. There has never been any proof, but tonight Wentworth asked about your brother—and the Spider killed him. No other living soul knew that your brother was informed of Ada Hamilton's whereabouts."

District Attorney Louis—the Fighting Bulldog they called him—lifted a hand and pressed it to his eyes. He looked again at Wentworth. "I still can't believe it," he said slowly. "Why Wentworth… Damn it, man, say something!"

Wentworth bowed, his face grave, and concerned. "I commiserate with you from the bottom of my heart," he said slowly. "As for this charge of Kirkpatrick's, that's his one obsession. He has been kind enough to think that my skill in handling criminal cases puts me in the same class with the Spider. I suppose it's logical. Had it ever occurred to you, Kirk, that the reason you can't prove the Spider and I are the same man is that—we are not?"

Kirkpatrick was looking at him with an eagerness he could not thrust out of his eyes.

"Wentworth," he said hesitantly. "Dick… I've never known you to break your word, or to lie about anything on earth to me. If you will give me your solemn word of honor…."

"Nonsense!" Wentworth said sharply. "I've had enough of these damned suspicions of yours! If you want to arrest me, go ahead, but for God's sake question Casaroma first! Don't you realize that Ada Hamilton's life hangs in the balance?"

The eagerness died out of Kirkpatrick's eyes. "You leave me no choice, Dick," he said slowly. "Evasions are all I ever get from you on that subject."

Louis was staring at him and a change crept over his face, too. Slow blood flushed darkly to his cheeks, ran into his temples. "By God," he snapped, "I believe you're right, Kirkpatrick. Wentworth, you'll burn for this if it's my last act! I swear it!"

Wentworth spun on him and anger leaped into his voice. "While you're throwing suspicions around, think about this. Some one revealed where Ada Hamilton was hidden. We three, and your brother, are the only ones who knew. One of us four… Or am I accused of conspiring with Casaroma also?"

"That will be enough, Wentworth!" Louis snapped. "My brother is dead—probably at your hands!"

The two men stood glaring at each other, no more than a few feet apart. Wentworth was conscious of Kirkpatrick's eyes upon him and they hurt.

"He's dead," Wentworth acknowledged. "For that, I am sorry. I believe in his honesty, but tell me this. Is it possible that someone had a hold over him? Is it possible that he gave the information to someone he trusted? Isn't it just possible that the Spider got his information from the other end of the line—from those that learned of Ada Hamilton's whereabouts and kidnaped her?"

Louis' fist struck out like lightning, but Wentworth merely pulled his head aside and allowed it to pass harmlessly over his shoulder.

"I see," he said quietly, "that you do consider it possible." He turned his back on Louis and faced Kirkpatrick. "Damn it, man, what have you done to find Ada Hamilton?"

Kirkpatrick's blue eyes regarded him steadily. "Casaroma insisted he knew nothing and his lawyers got him out on a writ before we had much chance to question him. Dick, I'm still waiting to hear you tell me, on your word of honor...."

"You won't hear it!" Wentworth snapped. "I'm fed up with these continual suspicions! If you won't do anything to find Ada...."

The door slapped open, and a man came pounding into Kirkpatrick's office.

The commissioner whirled to face him. "Kindly leave," he ordered coldly. "And in the future have yourself announced."

THE MAN strode up to Kirkpatrick. His height matched that of the dapper commissioner and his face was the weathered, wind-burned countenance of an outdoor man. There was a squared, belligerent thrust to his shoulders and his eyes were angry.

"I've been waiting for a half hour," he snapped, "and I don't propose to wait any longer. This is in line with all the other inefficiency of the police. I want a badge."

Kirkpatrick frowned at him but, before he could speak, Thomas Louis cut in, heavily. "It's all right, Kirkpatrick," he said. "This is Martin Meggs—a friend of mine. He's impetuous that way."

Meggs spun toward him. "What have you done to catch Delehanty's murderers?" He shouted, "By God, are you men or crawling dogs! If anyone in this man's town had two grains of courage or sense, this Spider would have been laid in a cell, where he belongs, years ago. Not that I intend to lay him there! Not while I've got two hands to avenge Dely!" He spun back to Kirkpatrick. "I've come to you, man-to-man, to ask for a badge to give me the legal right to hunt down the Spider. Not that I give a damn about the badge, but out of courtesy to you. And I'm kept waiting a half hour!"

Kirkpatrick shook his head, his lips unyielding. "We don't do things like that in New York," he said quietly, "and I'd advise you to let the law take its course. Or, if you have any information, turn it over to the police. I'll have to ask you to excuse me now, Mr. Meggs."

The man ripped out an explosive oath and went striding from the office. The door slammed terrifically behind him.

"Maybe you'd better hide me from him—like you did Ada Hamilton," Wentworth said dryly. "Only this time, don't tell so many people where you hide me."

Louis said furiously, "That will be enough from you, Wentworth. Martin Meggs is an honorable man—a soldier-of-fortune with more medals than he can hang on his chest. And he's my sister's fiancé. I won't have any two-bit crook...."

Wentworth bit out words. "I've heard all the insults I'm going to take from you, Louis. I've pardoned you up to now because I considered you distraught over your brother's death. I'm through. Kirkpatrick, if you're going to arrest me, get on with it and put me where I won't have to listen to this blind fool!" He was quite calm now.

"I told you that I was going to tap my sources of information in the Underworld tonight and see what I could learn. I've learned these things. The Underworld has a new master who calls himself the Whisper and has Chinese helpers—either a Chinese, or some man like this Martin Meggs just back from the wars—forgive that—it was a poor joke. I heard the whispers, then, that Ada Hamilton was to be kidnaped and that there was a leak in the district attorney's office." He frowned.

"What I can hear, the Spider can hear. It seems to me that you're making an arrest on damned flimsy grounds, but that's up to you. Get on with it."

Wentworth stood, angrily defiant, and watched Kirkpatrick's face. There was no relaxing of its stern lines.

"Give me your denial, Dick," he pleaded.

"Go to hell!" Wentworth snapped at him.

"Then I have no alternative. Richard Wentworth...."

The door of the office thrust open and a white-faced policeman stood on the threshold. His words came out in choked stammers.

"Forgive me, Commissioner," he gasped. "Forgive me, but... but they've found Ada Hamilton."

Wentworth sprang toward him. "Where, man?"

The policeman swallowed hard. "In Times Square. She was hanging on the news sign."

Wentworth flinched. That lovely girl, so brave... He heard Kirkpatrick's muffled curse. His voice rasped.

"Get on with it, Donovan."

"Yes, sir," the policeman whispered. "Yes, sir, I'm trying to. She didn't have nothing on and she was dead. She was all covered with… with burns and cuts and both arms and legs were broken and…."

Wentworth swore harshly, feeling fury run like fire through his veins. This was his own fault. If he had made Delehanty Louis talk….

"The ambulance doctor says she was—she was tortured to death."

In the silence that fell upon them there in the office, the whisper came startlingly loud, a whisper of sibilant, mocking laughter that seemed to come from everywhere and nowhere—the laughter of the Whisper of Doom!

"Thus die all enemies of the Whisper of Doom!"

CHAPTER 5
REIGN OF TERROR

WENTWORTH'S BRAIN had been numbed by the news of Ada Hamilton's tragic end. At the voice of the Whisper, he sprang into instant, violent action. He knew, automatically, that the Whisper had not come to police headquarters merely to deliver that mocking message. And Kirkpatrick stood in line with the open door through which the voice must be coming! He was striding angrily forward.

On the instant, Wentworth hurled himself at Kirkpatrick in a headlong tackle. His shoulder drove against the commissioner's thigh, battered him aside and, while they still were falling together to the floor, bedlam cut loose in the office. District Attorney Louis' voice rose in a hoarse shout. There was a tinkling crash of broken glass, and a man screamed. The scream rose tearing high, changed into a strangling groan. All that happened in that moment of time it took for Wentworth and Kirkpatrick to crash to the floor. But they were still in the direct path from the door.

In a quick lunge, Wentworth got on his knees, wrapped both arms around Kirkpatrick and surged toward the protection of a corner. Kirkpatrick was swearing, fighting his hold, but Wentworth's ears caught another sound—a groan and the heavy thick patter of liquid on the floor. Men's feet were slapping in the main hallway... There was no more whispering.

Slowly, Wentworth pushed to his feet. Kirkpatrick sprang up and took an angry step forward, then his eyes whipped toward the door. His head—then his whole body swung that way.

"Donovan!" he cried. "God in heaven, Donovan!"

Wentworth had no need to look at the policeman. His ears had told him the story. The slashing death of the Whisper of Doom had done its ghastly work, but this time it had caught its victim in the throat! Wentworth's eyes flashed to the district attorney, now just rising from behind the desk where he had crouched. Then Wentworth's gaze flicked beyond him to the broken window....

With a shout, Wentworth wheeled back toward the door, hurdled the crumpled body of Donovan and charged across the outer office. From behind him, Kirkpatrick's voice rang out.

"Halt! Halt, or I'll fire, Dick! You're under arrest!"

Wentworth did not check his speed, but the hall door

whanged inward and the opening was suddenly choked with men in police blue. He slammed into them before he could stop.

"Quickly!" he snapped. "A man murdered Donovan. The killer was in this hall. Search the building!"

"Halt!" Kirkpatrick shouted again. "Stand firm, men! I'm giving orders here." He came striding forward. "This time, your trickery won't work, Wentworth. You're not going to escape arrest!"

Wentworth turned on him furiously. "You blind fool!" he cried. "You're letting the murderer get away. Handcuff me, if you like, but let these men search right away. That attack was from inside the building."

"You lie," Kirkpatrick said calmly. "It came through the window."

Wentworth's face went white to the lips. His mouth shut in a bitter line. "Very well," he said quietly. "I lie—and the attack came through the window. That's why *all the broken glass is on the outside?*"

Kirkpatrick stared at him, frowning, took two quick strides to the door of his private office, then hurried back, swearing.

"Search every floor!" he shouted. "Bring all strangers here immediately, no matter what their excuses for being in the building!" He faced Wentworth. "I apologize Dick, but I still don't understand. Were there two knives thrown, and did one of them miss and go through the window? I'll have the street searched!"

Wentworth said, "I can't answer that one, but I don't think any thrown knife could do what the whispering death does." He walked slowly back to the inner office, forced himself to inspect the wound in Donovan's throat. It was a clean, deep cut, such as might be administered from behind by a powerful man wielding a razor-edged knife. He felt the muscles tighten across his shoulders, looked from the door to the spot where Kirkpatrick had been standing, then to the window.

Kirkpatrick, behind him, said solemnly, "You undoubtedly saved my life, Dick." His hand closed warmly on Wentworth's arm. "I wish… things were different, but…."

Wentworth's lips were twisted when they smiled "Go ahead with the arrest, Kirk," he said quietly.

District Attorney Louis, white and shaken beside Kirkpatrick's desk, came slowly forward.

"Kirkpatrick," he said, "we'll have to get that other Hamilton girl in a safer place. At any rate, we can't leave her in the home of… an accused murderer. We can't avoid arresting Wentworth. He practically convicts himself. How did he know what would happen when the whisper sounded?"

Wentworth stared at Louis and a slow doubt crept into him. The district attorney's question put it there. How had Louis known? For he had undoubtedly ducked behind the desk out of danger! Words sprang to Wentworth's lips, but he crushed them back. The action might have been instinctive, as his own was. It might have been….

Wentworth stood mute, while Kirkpatrick phoned to his men to go after the other Hamilton girl, to draw up an affidavit for Wentworth's arrest.

"Nita's on guard at the house," Wentworth said quietly. "You'll have to advise her what's happening. Otherwise, she won't open the gates even to police. The man who kidnaped Ada got in disguised as a policeman. I'd advise extraordinary precautions."

Kirkpatrick nodded briefly, and presently Wentworth was taken to a cell.

HIS BRAIN was tortured by a thousand doubts and questions. No doubt that the reign of terror of this Whisper of Doom had just begun—and powerfully. In one night, he had thrown the fear of torture and death into the Underworld and into the racket witnesses whom the district attorney had gathered. Overnight, the morale of criminals and gangsters would be stiffened. If the Whisper of Doom continued such activities, there would be such a crime wave as New York had never known before. And the witnesses—even the victims—would fear to talk!

Only one counter-stroke could be made, and it was a blow the law, itself, was powerless to deliver. The Whisper of Doom must be identified and given to justice. Wentworth's fine face drew into harsh lines. Against a criminal who could intimidate an entire city, the courts would be futile. It was for such work that the Spider had been born—to such tasks he had pledged his wealth and life. But now he lay, helpless, in the hands of the very man he wanted most to assist!

Well he knew the course he must follow when released. He must start a counter-reign of terror. The Spider must strike again and again until such time as he could track down this Whisper of Doom in his purple robe and devil's mask—and plant the scarlet seal of justice upon the unknown face behind it! Bitter, swift, unresting warfare must begin the moment Nita released him on a writ. Meanwhile, he must store up strength for the battle. Wentworth brought his powerful will to bear, drove worry from his brain and... slept.

He awoke abruptly, with the consciousness that someone was standing over him. He was instantly in full possession of his faculties. Years of peril had given him that power.

"Wake up, Wentworth," District Attorney Louis' voice said harshly.

Wentworth opened his eyes, sat up, quietly. Broad daylight was streaming into his cell. He saw Kirkpatrick, flanked by several men in police blue, at the door. Louis stood over him and staring up at his drawn face, Wentworth felt a sudden presentiment of disaster. He rose to his feet, dissimulating.

"You must pardon my seeming inhospitality," he said dryly, "but there are so few chairs. Won't you be seated?" He indicated his bunk.

"You cold-blooded villain!" Louis said hoarsely.

Wentworth swung toward Kirkpatrick. "You're damned inconsiderate of your guests, here," he said shortly. "I don't like to receive callers before breakfast."

Kirkpatrick looked at him with haggard eyes, and Wentworth felt his alarm mount.

Louis spoke raspingly. "A few hours ago, you told Kirkpatrick, in my presence, that Nita van Sloan was in charge of your house and that he would have to notify her of his intention to remove Frances Hamilton."

Wentworth's heart thudded violently. God, if they had seized

Frances, too! But this must be some new charge they were going to make against him.

"I also, if you will recall," he said flatly, "urged Kirkpatrick to take extraordinary precautions. What has happened?"

Kirkpatrick stepped quietly into the cell. "I pointed that out to you, Louis," he said. "I warn you I don't concur in your opinion of this."

Louis whirled on him. "Take care that I don't have you removed for conspiracy!" he shouted. "The men who kidnaped Frances Hamilton wore police uniforms! There have been too many men in police uniforms involved in this business!"

WENTWORTH'S QUICK mind instantly created the picture. Kirkpatrick had phoned a warning to Nita and, afterward, men in police uniform had called for the prisoner. She would release Frances Hamilton, naturally. But how in the name of Heaven had the Whisper of Doom learned what was impending? A wire-tap on his own home would do it, of course, but... Wentworth's eyes swung to Louis, and he recalled his fleeting suspicion of the man. Much simpler for Louis to have phoned a tip.

The district attorney was pounding on with his accusation of Kirkpatrick. "And in that other attack this morning, your police guards were withdrawn!"

Wentworth caught Louis' arm. "What other attack?" he demanded, his voice low.

Kirkpatrick's voice was flat with repressed emotion. "A witness against Gow, and Deputy District Attorney Lacrosse were killed by the Whisper this morning, when Lacrosse went to take the witness to court."

Wentworth ripped out an oath. Lacrosse had been Louis' chief assistant in all of his racket battles—also, he would be the first to suspect if Louis were crooked!

"Kirkpatrick!" Wentworth said, violently. "I've got to get out of here! Something has got to be done at once or this reign of terror will intimidate the entire city!"

Louis said softly, "So the Spider wants to go to work! Perhaps you'd like to put the seal on my forehead, too!"

Wentworth forced himself to calmness. "I can't answer for the Spider," he said slowly, "but it seems to me you're spending your time on wild-goose chases instead of getting actively to work against the Whisper. A case might be made out against you very easily."

Louis said with slow emphasis. "You won't get out of this cell. I'll fight you in every court, and there's no one to get you a writ. I've arrested all your accomplices. Jackson, that Hindu, your butler and your woman won't dare put in an appearance after turning Frances Hamilton over to the fake police—if that's what happened as your accomplices say."

Wentworth said incisively, "You will kindly refer to Miss van Sloan by her name or by her proper title. Miss van Sloan is my fiancée, understand?"

Louis' thick lips twisted into a sneer, but the stab of Wentworth's cold gray-blue gaze stopped words on his lips. Fear was a writhing, mighty thing in Wentworth's vitals. There was mean-

THOMAS LOUIS •

CASAROMA •

ing hidden behind Louis' words. Nita did not dare to put in an appearance. Nita… Wentworth's control snapped.

"For God's sake, Kirk," he cried. "What has happened to Nita?"

Kirkpatrick gazed at him bleakly. "I don't know, Dick," he said slowly. "The men who took Frances Hamilton away told Nita you wanted her at police headquarters. She went… with them."

Louis laughed harshly, "Do you still deny, Wentworth, that

you are allied with the Whisper—When your… your fiancée went away with them?"

Wentworth scarcely heard the district attorney's words. His eyes strained wide and wide with horror. Nita in the hands of the Whisper! In the hands of the torturers who had mangled Ada Hamilton until she died! A groan was wrenched out of Wentworth's heart. He sank down on the bunk and despair gripped his soul.

PHYLLIS LOUIS

MARTIN MIGGS

CHAPTER 6
DEATH AT HIS HEELS

THROUGH THE heaviness of his despair, the course he must follow flashed with photographic clarity into his mind. Every reason for freedom was accentuated a hundredfold by the fact that Nita's life was at stake. As Louis said, there was no one now to move for his release unless his lawyers acted on their own initiative when these facts were published. Louis would fight....

Through his fingers, Wentworth's wary eyes took in the grouping of the men before him. He could get through them, but would the door beyond be locked? It was a chance he must take. From utter collapse, Wentworth sprang into instantaneous, furious action. Legs crouched under him, he drove to the attack. A slicing blow with the side of his hand, striking throat nerve centers, spilled the district attorney unconscious to the floor. That was delivered in passing. Wentworth's shoulder caught Kirkpatrick in the solar plexus, hammered him back upon the three police grouped behind him in the doorway. Then Wentworth's hand darted to the commissioner's long-barreled revolver, yanked it clear!

Wentworth went on and through the three police with the impetus of his drive, in two strides reached the door that closed the end of the cell-gallery—and it was locked! Quicker than thought, the heavy revolver was leveled, and lead smashed into the tumblers. His shoulder hammered against the grating, and it clattered open. Behind him, a gun slammed, and he felt the pluck of lead beneath his arm. A long jump took him around a corner of the corridor a half-second ahead of a hurricane of bullets that *whanged* and whined off steel walls.

Feet beat out a tocsin on the metal floor plates, and a half-dozen alarm bells cut loose their violent clamor. But Wentworth moved through ways as familiar to him as his own home. He

56

was on top of the outer guard before the man could do more than clear his gun from its holster. A lightning blow dropped him, and Wentworth was free of the jail floor. He darted into a washroom, dropped out a window to the inner courtyard of the building. All of this happened swiftly.

In two bounds he was beside a motorcycle parked there. He kicked up its stand and ran with it toward the gateway. The motor caught; he vaulted to the saddle and went roaring through the city streets. Futile to go to his own home, and police radio cars would trap him quickly if he stayed on the motorcycle. Within a dozen blocks, he abandoned the machine and walked hurriedly to the nearest elevated station. Only one refuge was open to him. Bereft of all his comrades, and even of Nita's loving support, hunted by police and Underworld alike, Richard Wentworth must vanish. In his place would be… Blinky McQuade!

Bitterly, Wentworth grudged the minutes it took him to reach the sleazy room of Blinky McQuade and slip unobserved into its refuge. Swiftly, he opened a secret cache in the thick, high headboard of the bed and got out make-up materials and clothing. Ten minutes later, Blinky McQuade shuffled out into the squalor of Holian Alley and turned his footsteps west and north—toward the home of Mike Casaroma!

UNDER WENTWORTH'S arms were two guns from the Holian Alley cache; around his waist was a leather-pouched girdle of tools and he carried in a bundle the long black cape and slouch hat of the Spider. If he were ever searched by a suspicious policeman, he was doomed—but it was necessary. Now was no time for reckless hunting of clues, the slow tracing down of

the kidnapers' movements. He must
strike directly at the head, force the
truth from Casaroma. Otherwise,
Nita and Frances Hamilton would
die terribly.

On the way uptown by subway,
Wentworth skimmed through a newspaper. It was all there—
all that he had feared and more! "Reign of Terror... New City
Administration Terrorized... Leak in Prosecutor's Office..."
Across one front page ran a screaming editorial attack on the
inefficiency, or complicity, of the police. District Attorney Louis'
brother was called a martyr to good government, and once more
the cry of *Death to the Spider* screamed from every column.

Slowly, Wentworth balled the paper and dropped it to the
floor and there was a weary, bitter twist to his mouth. So it was
always that the best efforts of the Spider were rewarded; but
it did not matter. The service he rendered was its own recom-
pense—that and the happiness among the people for whom
he fought. Behind the disguising hooded spectacles of Blinky
McQuade, he closed his eyes to plan. Any way in which he
entered Casaroma's stronghold would be fraught with peril, but
it must be done....

Blinky McQuade had donned his meager best for this excursion among the upper crust of crookdom, but the guards at
the entrance of the apartment building glared at him hostilely.
There were many more than there had been last night—whether
because of the Spider's invasion or because it was normal prac-
tice in broad daylight such as this, Wentworth did not know.

Wentworth cringed before them servilely as Blinky would. "I gotta see the big shot," he mumbled, "or anyway somebody close to him. You just phone them that Blinky McQuade's here and he's gotta talk to somebody about something important."

The broad-shouldered guard sneered at Blinky's humbleness, but sent up the message as requested, and a few moments later Wentworth was speeding upward in an elevator. A cold-eyed lieutenant of Casaroma saw him.

"Look, Mr. Domico," Blinky said huskily, "I was down to Balmy's last night when this here Whitey Morgan was killed. The Billikin was there, too, him what the Spider killed later on."

Domico's eyes were unwinking. "So," he said.

"What I got to tell the big shot is this," Blinky went on, hurriedly. "I saw a guy following the Billikin when he left. I got me a hunch maybe he was the Spider!"

Domico's eyes narrowed. "So," he said softly. "Who'd you see?"

Wentworth still cringed, but there was a stubborn slyness in his voice. "I want to tell the big shot, myself," he said. "Then maybe when he needs a good safecracker, he'll deal me in on the job. It ought a be worth something to have a guess at who the Spider is."

Domico took out a wallet and tossed two bills on the desk before him. "There's two C's. Now spill it and I'll see the big shot knows who brought it."

Wentworth took the money, cringingly, "But I'd like to see the big shot!" he whined.

Domico came around the desk in two feral strides. "You don't want to see the big shot," he said softly.

Wentworth stumbled in his apparent eagerness to get away from the man. "Sure, I don't!" he cried. "Sure, I was just fooling. I'd much rather tell you, Mr. Domico. Look, this guy that followed the Billikin was a Chink—honest to God!" Rapidly, he sketched a description of the Chinese he had killed in the battle on the roof.

"You wouldn't kid me, Blinky," Domico said slowly. "I know you wouldn't kid me." His eyes were opening and there was a shallow, cruel look in them. "You wouldn't do that."

"So help me God!" Wentworth cried.

Domico paused, then shrugged. "Okay, beat it. I'll see that the big shot knows you brought the news. Go on. Scram."

WENTWORTH GRINNED placatingly with Blinky McQuade's loose-lipped, trembling mouth, backed toward the door. He stumbled against a gunman and got kicked hard. Raucous laughter followed him; as he ran out of the door. Once that portal swung shut behind him, his manner changed to swift efficiency. He snatched up the bundle he had deposited out there and dodged toward the fire-stairs. Its fourth wall was open and from it he peered across to the terrace of Casaroma's penthouse. It was guarded by spiked steel, but as he looked a slow smile came to Wentworth's lips. This was the easy part of it.

A steel wedge, with protruding spines, secured the door against invasion from this floor, and rapidly he donned the wig, hat and cape of the Spider. He doubled a length of the silken web, cast it over one of the steel spikes and quickly knotted it so that it formed a double rope between the metal railing of the fire-stairs and the spike-guard of the penthouse. It would be easy to withdraw the web from either end merely by pulling on one side of the loop until the knot was within reach. A moment he peered downward into the twenty stories of emptiness below— searched the windows of the building to see that he was unobserved. Then, he swung off into space!

A half-dozen hand-over-hand swings put him in reach of the guard and a rapid vault took him over. He hesitated over the web then slowly drew the knot to him, unfastened it and recoiled the silken robe in its pocket of the cape. If he left hurriedly, this route would not suffice. If he had leisure, he could reconstruct his rope escape. He faced about toward the terrace of Casaroma's home, made his furtive way in the shadow of its wall. Luckily, the terrace was not overlooked by any other, but still this daylight work was not to the Spider's liking.

Four windows opened in the wall along which Wentworth crept. One was open a few inches and toward that he moved rapidly, paused as words came faintly to him in a voice he recognized—the husky, oily voice of Casaroma. It was lifted, angrily.

"Sure, I know I owe you plenty! Sure! But the *Britannie* is just plain damned foolish. The answer is 'no!'"

Wentworth heard the mechanic rattle of a phone slamming back into its cradle. The words didn't make sense to him, but that didn't matter. He had located his man, and as for the rest… From his pocket, Wentworth slipped a minute periscope, with a panoramic mirror, and, through its use, peered unobserved into the room.

Casaroma's wide back was toward the window and within a

yard of it. He was sitting behind a huge desk and his hands were clamped on its edge with a fury that whitened the knuckles.

"Domico!" he bellowed, and the man to whom Wentworth had spoken popped into the room. "You tell them guards downstairs not to let another soul in—not one. This here Whisper guy has gone crazy."

Domico nodded and jerked out of the door again. Casaroma jumped to his feet and began to pace the office. Wentworth was afire with impatience, and realized it would be impossible to make an entrance, unnoticed. Best to get Casaroma away from his desk where it would be harder for him to signal. With a single deft movement, Wentworth had an automatic in his hand. He slipped the periscope away and drew in a slow, tense breath. *Now!*

A hand thrust up the window, and the automatic was yawning into Casaroma's startled face.

"One word," Wentworth said quietly, "and you die—*under the Spider's seal!*"

CASAROMA'S FAT jowls quivered and his swarthy face slowly turned a dirty gray. He didn't speak as Wentworth hooked a leg over the sill and went inside, smoothly. He angled past the racketeer and locked the door, set his shoulders against it.

"It's time," he said softly, "that you and I had a talk. Don't you think so, Casaroma? I should have put your number up long ago."

Casaroma was fighting for his usual cold self-complacence, but Wentworth did not intend to let him regain it. The man was shaken, and if he were crowded now....

Wentworth moved toward him, the gun in one fist. Swiftly, he scooped out his cigarette lighter and thumbed open its base.

"This is a thing no man has ever seen and lived to talk about," he said. "This is the way the seal is put on—the seal of the Spider, Casaroma, for those whom the Spider kills!"

Casaroma's legs seemed to turn to rubber. He sagged into a big chair and words stuttered to his lips. "*Santa Maria*," he whispered. "*Santa Maria dulcie....*"

In Italian, Wentworth answered him. "It's rather late to call on the Virgin now, but perhaps she can save you... if you will give me the knowledge to save the two women the Whisper stole for you!"

Casaroma's thick hands flew out in a hopeless gesture. "I do not know," he stammered. "Santa Maria hear me, I do not know! Over the phone, the Whisper says to me, 'Do this for me and you shall have this other witness. Do not do it, and I shall return her to the police.' Of this other woman of whom you speak, I know nothing—*nothing!*"

Wentworth choked back a violent oath. In the man's trembling fear, he recognized the accents of truth. And it was a game the Whisper would play, if, as Wentworth had suspected throughout, the man was not a member of the Underworld over which Casaroma kinged it, but an outsider muscling in. Yes, it had the earmarks of truth. But Nita....

Hope surged through him. "He will keep this witness alive then?" he said swiftly to Casaroma.

Casaroma's head sagged in assent. Might it not be, then, that he had seized Nita to obtain a hold over Wentworth? Already, his tapped wires, or whatever secret source of information he possessed, would have told him that the police believed Wentworth and the Spider were one. Something of the lightening of his fury must have shown in his face, for Casaroma's head lifted slightly.

"Still, there are things you can tell me," Wentworth said and once more his tones held the biting menace of the Spider. "For instance, this job that the Whisper bids you do. This thing that is crazy—the *Britannie.*"

Casaroma gestured eagerly. "It is madness. I refuse to do it. I bar my doors to him, and...."

A sibilant whisper cut across his voice, the Whisper of Doom! *"Death waits for those who talk!"* it said. *"Death to the Spider!"*

From all about Wentworth, the whisper seemed to come, and there flashed across his mind the picture of those who had died under the mocking laughter of that voice—at the blow of this weapon which could not be seen and which left no after trace save death!

CHAPTER 7
MURDER MADNESS

A S THE first whispered word reached his ears, Wentworth sprang into violent action. It would be impossible to think out a plan in such brief heartbeats of time, and yet Wentworth moved with the precision of machinery—and moved right. He had his gun in his hand, twisted and fired straight at the open window. He went toward Casaroma in a headlong dive. He heard a hard-driven missile hiss past his head and there was a crash and tinkle of breaking glass. Laid over all that, rang the wild laughter of the Whisper.

All this happened in the instant that it took Wentworth's leap to reach Casaroma. His attack drove the racketeer back into the depths of his chair as he surged to his feet, carried man and chair crashing to the floor. Wentworth sprawled beyond, on hands and feet, still clutching his automatic. He seized Casaroma by the throat.

"Talk, and talk fast," he whispered, "or I'll put you up where the Whisper can kill you. He's angry over that turndown!"

Casaroma shook like lumpy jelly under the threat of the Spider's cold words, ready gun. Outside the door, men were shouting. Death for the Spider, was perhaps only minutes away, but death was even closer for Casaroma, and he knew it.

"He wanted me—" Casaroma barely breathed the words—"to rob the *Britannie* of gold."

Wentworth stared at the man and felt coldness run along his spine. No wonder Casaroma had shouted that it was a crazy plan. The *Britannie* was France's largest, fastest liner, and… Good God! The payment on the war debts! France, perhaps timorous at the growing tensity of the threatening war situation, was making a friendly gesture toward the United States. She would pay in gold, and the shipment was soon due in. No one would be told, of course, when it would arrive, but it would surely come on the *Britannie*. She was docking tonight.

Wentworth's hand tightened on the butt of his automatic. One bullet now, into Casaroma's skull… The racketeer read the Spider's tautening face and squealed with terror. It was not mercy that stayed Wentworth's hand. He had never yet shot down a helpless man in cold blood. It was the Spider's code, indefensible in cold logic, to give even the lowest criminal an even break. But if he could believe that killing Casaroma would stop the raid on the *Britannie,* no scruple would stay his hand. The truth was that, alive, Casaroma was a greater obstacle to the Whisper's plans than if he were slain.

His resolution formed, Wentworth hesitated no longer. A slap of the gun barrel knocked Casaroma senseless. Only seconds had passed since that first warning whisper. Outside the door, men still clamored and shouted. Soon they would break it down—and outside the window was the Whisper with its flashing, unseeable death. If he could kill the Whisper....

Wentworth heaved up the heavy chair and carried it before him like a shield; rested its seat upon his head and twisted it so that he could just see. Gun in hand, he moved steadily toward the window. His lips were drawn into a harsh line, pressed coldly against Ms teeth. His eyes were bitter gray.

"Whisper!" he called clearly. "Whisper, the Spider comes to fight you to the death!"

And swiftly the answer came! Mocking laughter... and where sunlight slanted through the window, something flashed with a cold glitter! Wentworth flinched back, but it was the chair which saved him. Within a hairbreadth of his throat, a cleanly sliced furrow, inches deep, suddenly appeared upon the leather arm! Death had been that close! Wentworth did not hesitate. With a shout, he slammed the chair against the window. He felt a double jar, as more missiles thudded against it. One sliced entirely through, hissed hungrily past him—and Wentworth took his risk! He whipped the chair to one side and dived head-first through the window!

IN THAT first flashing moment, when his eyes swept the terrace, Wentworth realized that only a miracle could save him! Four men had weapons trained on him—four men in gorgeous purple robes and devil masks! Wentworth realized that their weapons, which resembled powerful cross-bows, would concentrate on him the deadly missiles that killed hideously... like mighty knives. Even then, Wentworth might successfully fight them, if they were closely grouped, but their leader, the Whisper, had been too wise for that. They stood at four widely separated points. So much Wentworth saw as he fell, curling head and shoulders under for a tumbler's landing on the roof. He heard the Whisper's hissing order.

"Hold your fire until he lands—then all together!"

Anguish was bitter in Wentworth's heart. It was not that he feared death—even so horrible a death. It was the realization that, with his demise, Nita, too, would be doomed since there no longer would be reason for keeping her alive. The Whisper would regain full ascendency over Casaroma; the *Britannie* would be looted with awesome loss of life. If only he knew which of these men was the Whisper! Their identical costumes and weapons gave him no clue. The sound of the whisper, itself, might come from anyone of them. To kill the Whisper, the Spider would be willing to die!

Wentworth moved with the celerity of a golf ball striking

rock. Shoulders scarcely touched the roof before he had bounded to his feet and was running violently toward the nearest of the men! His gun blasted viciously in his hand and he remembered to shoot for the throat. The impact of the lead hurled the man violently backward, head wrenched excruciatingly between his

The masked figure was
hurled violently backward
by the lead impact.

shoulders. The crossbow flew high. But now the other three men fired! Only Wentworth's incredibly fleet movement saved him from that first volley. There was a jerk that sliced off the crown of his hat, cleanly. A jagged tear appeared in his cape, but he was still racing on toward the man he had slain. If he could reach the body and use it for a shield....

The three men had dropped their crossbows and snatched up others propped against then legs—but, in the interval, Wentworth fired again! In his swift running, he miscalculated slightly. The man at whom he fired reeled back a step, wavered on his feet, but the cross-bow swung up relentlessly. Wentworth sprang into the air again, diving headfirst. Too late he realized his mistake. He was as easy target as a straight-flying bird but he did not have a bird's facility for dodging! He heard the sibilant laughter ring out. Desperately, Wentworth balled his body, purling his head between hunched shoulders, reaching downward for the floor. His foot struck, dragged. He landed heavily on his shoulder, and brought up against the body of the dead killer.

Gravel spurted into his face and a thin line burned across his ear. He felt the warm rush of blood. But he had reached his goal. With a frenzy of strength, he heaved the body half upright before him and from that cover his gun blasted. The first shot was wild, a feeble effort to disconcert the killers. The second was deliberate, and the robed man spun, staggered against the low balustrade that skirted its edge. He screamed, terribly, before he pitched over into space. Wentworth's gun was seeking new targets—but suddenly there were none!

INCREDIBLY, IN that brief moment while he heaved up

his corpse shield, the other two robed figures had vanished! Did that mean he had killed the Whisper? With frantic hope, Wentworth wrenched at the devil mask on the man he held, tore it loose and cursed his disappointment. The man was a low-caste Chinese. Those features held no hint of an intelligence equal to the ghastly work of the Whisper!

But there was no safety here for him. Within moments, those men of Casaroma would stream out of the terrace doors. Only the urgency of reaching their chief had delayed them until now. With vicious force, Wentworth applied the Spider's seal to the forehead of the dead Chinese, then he was on his feet, dashing directly at the penthouse!

The French doors stood open on a drawing-room and he catapulted through them. A portiere parted in half, sliced cleanly through, by the whispering death, as he dashed past. He flung a wild shot at a dark doorway, but could not know if his enemy lurked there. Straight across the room he charged, into a hallway, through a door—and found himself once more in the corridor outside Casaroma's apartment.

Instantly, Wentworth flung himself at the steps. Upstairs, was the Whisper, himself, and one of his men. The Spider still might trap them. He would not flee—yet his own death in the encounter was too likely for him to risk that without first summoning men who might succeed if he failed. Without hesitancy, he shot the lock off an apartment door and rushed inside. Distantly, he heard a woman screaming, but paid it no heed. A telephone! He snatched it up, flung the police emergency number into the mouthpiece. It would connect him directly with Kirkpatrick's private office. Almost with a sob of relief, he heard the cool crisp tones of the commissioner.

"Kirkpatrick," Wentworth snapped, and his voice was the flat mocking voice that the world identified with the Spider, "I am in Casaroma's apartment house. The Whisper is here, too. I have killed two of his men, but the rest are here. I am going up to fight them, but send as many police as you can—in case I fail. And if I fail, I will be dead, so heed this warning, if you never heeded one from me before. The *Britannie* is bringing the French war debt payment. The Whisper is planning to rob the ship. It must be prevented."

Without waiting for an answer, Wentworth slammed up the receiver and dashed back into the hall. The whole business of phoning Kirkpatrick had taken perhaps a minute and yet now absolute silence reigned save for the continued screaming of the woman behind him. Furiously, Wentworth flung himself at the stairs. Surely, they had not abandoned the battle!

Wentworth raced into Casaroma's apartment through the open door and, with a heavy roar, a double-barreled shotgun blasted almost in his face. The wind of the discharge sent him reeling against the wall, but it had missed him clean. His speed of entrance had saved him! Still staggering from the concussion, Wentworth sprinted on through the apartment.

Doors stood open, but nowhere was there any trace of the Whisper or of Casaroma's gangsters. He darted to Casaroma's office. Confound it, there was trickery here. Somewhere they had set a trap… abruptly, Wentworth smiled. Of course. The trap would be sprung below, when he attempted to leave the building. It was an obvious course. Instead of hunting him down and facing his deadly guns, they would lie in ambush, below!

Wentworth snatched up a telephone from Casaroma's desk and once more called headquarters. "Send those police silently, Kirkpatrick," he said swiftly. "I'm in the penthouse, and somewhere below, the Whisper is setting an ambush."

Kirkpatrick's voice came raspingly back to him. "That's done, already. Listen to me, Wentworth or Spider or whoever you are. You have never lied to me. Delehanty Louis... was he guilty?"

"He confessed telling some one where Ada Hamilton was hidden," Wentworth said slowly. "And this is truth, too. Before he could tell me the rest, he tried to shoot me. But he was shot by one of the Whisper's men. It was not I who killed him. Kirkpatrick, the whispering death is some sort of missile fired from cross-bows. Apparently, they can't be fired rapidly. Good-by, and don't forget the *Britannie!*"

QUICKLY, WHEN he had hung up, Wentworth found a mirror and before it he performed the transformation back into the cringing Blinky McQuade. Regretfully, he made a bundle of torn Spider cape and tools, even of guns—for one of them would match with the slug that had killed a man who bore the Spider seal. Using a short length of the silken rope, he whirled the bundle rapidly around his head and hurled it far out toward Central Park. He saw it fall beyond the wall, perhaps secure until he could reclaim it, then he assumed Blinky McQuade's shuffling gait and puttered down the long flights of steps toward the first floor.

He was on the sixth floor when police found him, cowering

in a porter's closet, and he was hauled up before Kirkpatrick. But they were looking for bigger game than small-time crooks who had come to sell information to Casaroma. They had found the ambuscade—three men armed with automatics and a machine gun—but of Casaroma, himself, and the Whisper there was no trace. When the captives sneeringly confirmed Blinky's story, he went free. Within minutes, he had recovered his precious bundle and was racing once more through the city, bent on battle with the Whisper.

Of only one thing could he be sure now. The Whisper would compel Casaroma to go forward with his attack on the *Britannie*. Also, the Whisper would be there. Those of the Whisper's men who escaped would flee to his hiding place. The Spider would follow and there he might find and release Nita and Frances Hamilton. There would be justice for the Whisper— and freedom for Nita.

His course was plain. He must be there when the Whisper struck, and there was only one way to accomplish that. He must get hold of a plane. His home would be a police trap, but he must walk into it, steal his amphibian from the secret hangar beneath the pier and speed eastward. There were hidden machine guns built into his amphibian. He would need them.

On wealthy Sutton Place, Blinky McQuade would be a conspicuous figure. Besides, if he were spotted, he did not wish Blinky McQuade to be identified with Richard Wentworth. A slight grim smile touched Wentworth's lips. No, the only man he could afford to have seen entering Wentworth's home, escaping in Wentworth's plane was—Richard Wentworth himself!

Sardonically, he used the money received from Casaroma's lieutenant to purchase suitable clothing which he donned in a subway washroom. He was burning with impatience, but restrained himself. It would be some time before the Whisper could put his plans into effect and once Wentworth stole the plane, he would be marked. Every landing field and seaplane port would be watched for him. He regretted bitterly the day's failure. He had been face to face with the Whisper—yet the Whisper had escaped. It was no mitigation in Wentworth's mind, that the Whisper had fled. Somewhere, the Spider had failed miserably or that escape would not have been possible. Because he had failed, the warfare must go on, innocents must suffer, and Nita....

Wentworth closed his mind on the thought. He dared not think of her lest he quail in battle, for mere triumph over the Whisper would not be enough to save her! Wentworth ate a hurried meal, bought a newspaper—and stared with anger pumping through his entire being. From the front page stared up at him the photograph of Martin Meggs, under a headline—

SOLDIER OF FORTUNE SWEARS
TO KILL SPIDER IN REVENGE

And there was another, more menacing story that stabbed him to the heart. Screaming type stated that a whispering voice, terming itself the "Whisper of Doom" had phoned the newspaper.

"I have a warning to Richard Wentworth, the Spider," said the voice—the news story ran—"Unless he surrenders to the police within twenty-four hours, someone else will pay the penalty for him. I think he will understand the message."

Wentworth understood, and it shook him as nothing in his warfare with this powerful criminal had done. Nita was definitely in his power, and, unless he surrendered to the police, Nita would share Ada Hamilton's fate! He had no doubt at all that the threat would be fulfilled—if he failed to surrender. And yet, if he went to a cell, who would rescue Nita? Well he knew that, whether he surrendered or not, she was doomed. For, once he was in police hands, there no longer was any reason to keep her alive.

Wentworth came stiffly to his feet. He could delay no longer. Heaven help any of the Whisper's men who fell into the Spider's hands this day! Heaven help any who opposed his deliberate plan. He intended to walk openly into his home where police would be waiting in ambush for him....

CHAPTER 8
EXCURSION TO HELL

THE EXCURSION boat, *S. S. Happiness*, swam placidly up the bay through waters turned strangely sullen and red by the flame of the setting sun. Broad-beamed, homely as a brooding duck, she mothered her crowded load of humanity. Children screamed and ran in unending nameless games. Families sat sprawled out under the lee of the cabins. They were happy and safe... at present.

One child-weary matron leaned toward another. "Seems like

there's a lot more men coming back from the picnic than went down."

The other woman sniffed. "Don't look to me like honest, church-going folk neither. Beats all what the pastor will do to keep from having a deficit—letting the likes of *them* aboard!"

"Sure, it's that flighty young wife of the pastor's... Junior, keep away from that railing!"

Women, comfortably gossiping, not really worried about the strange number of men that didn't look like "church-going folk." How those men would have laughed at that! And some of that laughter would have been sibilant, *whispering....*

A series of small excited cries rippled over the decks. Children, men and young couples began to move to the port side to gaze on the great glistening liner overtaking the *S. S. Happiness.* On the boat deck, where young lovers sat close together and impatiently awaited the dusk, a boy put a furtive arm about a girl.

"That big boat's the *Britannie,*" he murmured, "the biggest, fastest ship in the world. Maybe she'll go on a summer cruise. Maybe, baby, if we both save our money...."

The girl laughed. "Silly, I'm saving my money for furniture— *our* furniture."

"Our furniture!"

They forgot it was not yet dusk; but the girl, of that other couple forward, was timid.

"Please, Tom, everyone can see... Oh, look, some men going into the pilothouse! I didn't know you were allowed to!"

"You ain't," the boy said flatly. "Sit down!"

"But I want to go in, too! Pretty please, Tommy."

Tom slouched toward the pilot-house and knocked on the door. It slid open, a few inches. A man glared out.

"Scram, punk!" he ordered raspingly.

Tom bristled, but the girl plucked nervously at his arm. "Come away, Tommy," she whispered. "That man... He looks like he'd kill you for two cents!"

Actually, the man's wage for murder was a bit higher. His rock-bottom price was fifty dollars.

"Look, Tom, we're going closer to that big ship. Oh, I hope we don't go *too* close!"

Tom's hand closed on hers, "I'd take care of you, honey...."

The people on the port deck were pleased that the *S. S. Happiness* was veering so close to the *Britannie*, whose great steel side could crush its timbers like tinder. There would be time for rescues, of course, in case of collision—for a few rescues. Men, at least, could swarm up the ropes and ladders the *Britannie* would lower. Men who were ready and knew what would happen. But not victims who....

Aboard the *Britannie*, an excited officer jabbered at the pilot. "No," he replied, "those excursion boats don't carry radio. You might try sounding your siren."

The great bass siren of the *Britannie* thundered out its staccato warning. The reedy note of the *Happiness* answered as pipingly as a tug, but its course remained unchanged.

"The damned fools!" the pilot swore. "We can't turn aside here. The channel's narrow, and with this craft's draft...." He stepped to the megaphone with its microphone amplifier, and his magnified voice went thundering across the water. "Sheer off, *Happiness,* or our suction will pull you in!"

A radio man darted to the bridge. "Radio from that plane up there, sir. Says robbers we were warned about may be on that excursion boat. Advises us to stand off."

"Stand off in this narrow channel!" The pilot shouted again into the microphone. "You fools, veer off or we'll crash!"

There was dead silence on the decks of the *Happiness* now. In sudden terror, men and women shrank back from the rail. The sides of the *Britannie* towered, mountainous, above them. On the boat deck, Tom was staring, white-faced, toward the pilot-house.

"Something's wrong in there," he said. "I'm going to find out what it is!"

The girl clung to his arm, but he shook her off. He was angry over that curt call-down. He ripped open the door. A hand reached out, and he was yanked inside. He made no sound, but on the deck the girl's voice lifted in a clear, soaring scream. A hundred voices answered hers—voices of panic....

LOUDER AND higher even than those screams came the wind-shriek of a diving plane. Its engine raved at full throttle, and at its stick crouched a man whose face was grim and white. Across his temple was a streak of blood and a bandage was on his left wrist—the cost of stealing the plane. His lips moved in silent curses.

Minutes ago, Richard Wentworth was telling himself, he should have realized the meaning of the converging courses of those two boats—the mighty *Britannie* and that pitiful little white chip beside it, the *S.S. Happiness.*

He could see men and women running on her decks, specks of doomed humanity. At the stern of the *Britannie,* the water was lashed to a white foam by reversed screws, but it would take more than that to stop those thousands of tons of steel. The *Happiness* still might swerve aside, but instead her bow now turned more sharply toward the *Britannie,* and her stern showed only the placid wake of an excursion boat on a pleasure cruise.

With a steadiness that told nothing of his tortured doubts, Wentworth's hand moved to a button, and small ports in the motor cowling slid open. Behind them were the gaping muzzles of machine guns. Innocent men might be in that pilot-house. The steering gear might have jammed—but in that case why had not the engines been reversed? Surely, both mechanisms couldn't have gone wrong!

A hundred yards away, Wentworth leveled off his amphibian, skimming low above the water. He saw the door of the pilot-house yank open, and a man's body tossed to the deck. Wentworth's eyes became furious slits. No longer could there be any doubt. Carefully, he eased back the stick until the cross-hairs of his gun sights centered on that closing door. Only such a superb marksman as the Spider could have risked this kind of shooting. But there were beads of cold perspiration on his forehead as he jammed his thumbs home on the trigger trips of his machine guns! He must not risk failure now.

It was a desperate chance he was taking, but he knew that in so small a boat as the *Happiness,* there would be pressure on the rudder from such a sharp turn. If the wheel were released, there would be a back-lash that would swing its nose off that deadly course. There should be… He saw the greasy smoke of his tracers streak grayly toward his target, then glass leaped from the windows of the pilothouse. The door whipped open and a man, bounding out, was caught in mid-flight by screaming steel. His body hammered back against the bulkhead, pinned there in the flashing moment that Wentworth's lead streamed from gun muzzles, then collapsed bloodily to the deck. He would perform no more fifty-dollar murders….

The next instant, Wentworth was forced to yank the stick back. His amphibian leaped clear of the house, wheeled in a sharp *virage* that missed the masts by a handbreadth. Instantly, he was banking again to a landing upon the waters that were so sullen and red with sunset. Now a gasp of hope squeezed out between Wentworth's stiff lips. The wake of the *Happiness* had altered—*away from the Britannie!*

Hope died at its birth. His intercession had come too late. The *Happiness* was turning away, but already the suction of that huge, floating city had caught its frail hulk. Now Wentworth's pontoons took the water, and his plane skidded toward the *Happiness*. He heard above his dying motors, as if a steam-roller were grinding over an orange crate, a slow, splintering crash!

For an instant, he heard screams, and then the thunderous, booming distress signal of the *Britannie* went echoing across the waters and blotted out all other sound. The *Happiness* reeled away from the collision, was sucked remorselessly back. It seemed but half a boat, its side ground in by the rasping steel plates, a buzz-saw eating into cheese. Ropes, ladders, life-preservers rained upon the churning waters from the *Britannie*. Boats swung out from its davits. From the *Happiness*, human bodies arched out into space. Women screamed into the bedlam and children's terrified voices piped thinly. Up those ropes that led to the *Britannie's* deck, men were swarming—Men who did not look like church-going folk.

ON THAT shattered boat deck, a girl's body lay across the fallen form of a boy named Tom. There was a bloody gash on his scalp. The girl's head lay against an iron stanchion. The funnel, old-fashioned and high, lay across the huddled bodies of two others who were wrapped in each other's arms. It did not matter now for what they had saved their money. On a lower deck, already awash with the rising sea, a woman screamed for a boy who did not answer, would never answer. He had gone to the port deck to see the big ship.

Before her eyes, a plane that floated upon the water slued to a jarring halt and a man leaped to the wing, ran along it to the deck. He smiled at her and his smile was curiously gentle for all the stiff tension of his cheeks.

"If you'll step to the wing, madam," he said, "you'll be safe enough. A life-preserver first…" He reached overhead and snaked a jacket from a rack, fitted it hurriedly to her. "Even if you fall overboard, you'll float like a cork," he told her. "Help is coming."

He lifted his voice and its clearness cut across the muddle of panic. "Life-preservers! Get on life-preservers and jump overboard. Paddle away from the boat. Help is coming. You'll be entirely safe. Jump overboard with life-preservers!"

Nothing of the frantic need for haste seeped through into his voice. There was a lurch of the deck beneath his feet, a sharp settling, and from aft there came a muffled explosion. More screams and then, terribly clear against the encroaching dusk, the red glare of... *of fire!*

Wentworth worked with frantic speed, shouting, thrusting panicky women into life-preservers, binding them tightly about small bodies that trembled to his touch. Where he moved, screaming stopped and a semblance of order followed. A child looked up into his face and smiled tremulously while tears still coursed down his cheeks.

"I want Mama," he confided.

"She'll be found," Wentworth told him cheerfully. She might be found, but only God knew whether living or dead! "Now I'm going to throw you into the water, just like down at the beach. You know, paddle with your hands and feet away from the boat. It'll be fun!"

"Fun."

Wentworth caught up the child. "Remember, paddle!" He tossed him out into the water, saw him bob up, frightened again, crying out, but paddling, paddling... The deck here was clear, and aft the avid flames licked higher. Wentworth sprang to the railing, caught the scupper overhead and swung himself to the deck above. The flames were wilder here on dry decks. And death was everywhere. The boat listed heavily. Two hundred yards away, the *Britannie* had finally come to a halt and, at anchor, was sending back a swarm of boats. Toward the shore, Wentworth could see a dozen flying specks, planes racing toward them. The wireless must have been busy… or else they were the men of the Whisper.

Rage distorted Wentworth's face. God, the man who could conceive such horror as this for his own selfish ends could not be human! And the looting of the *Britannie* would be ridiculously easy. All her crew would be overboard, fishing the drowning from the sea. Those men who had swarmed up the first ropes would be Casaroma's killers! Had they won?

But now was no time for the Spider's vengeance. First of all, he served humanity, and about him people were pitifully dying. He had a glimpse of his own plane, as he sprang to further rescue work. Its wings were loaded with women and children and, on the low-pressed hull, men labored to lift others from the water. But it would carry so pitifully few and there were so many, so many others….

The decks slanted so steeply that Wentworth must find handholds in order to climb, pass out life-preservers, throw the panic-stricken overboard to the comparative safety of the water. Only a few minutes at most before the *Happiness* dived to the bottom. Over everything spread the red menacing glare of the fire. Great tongues of it billowed upward. Black smoke swirled stranglingly along the deck and somewhere a woman screamed in burning agony, trapped and tortured.

Furiously, Wentworth fought toward the sound. Under him, the ship shuddered and slipped lower into the water.

"Jump!" he shouted. "Jump overboard! She's going!"

He toiled on up the steepening deck. Through the strangling smoke, he saw the woman, penned in a small room whose window was to small for her body. An ax… Wentworth smashed a glass pane with an elbow and yanked it out.

"Get back!" he shouted at the woman. "Get back!"

She screamed into his face and did not hear. Frantically, Wentworth leaped toward her. He jabbed stiffened fingers into her throat and she sagged, unconscious, across the sill. The ax crashed into wood… A lurch threw Wentworth a half-dozen feet away, and flame gushed at him. A cry burst from his lips, and he sprang back to the work. The ax made a glittering circle of red light, as he whirled it. A man's voice took up his cry.

"Overboard. Overboard! *She's going!*"

A LAST slashing blow of the ax severed the casement, and Wentworth seized it with his hands, ripped it free. A violent heave brought the woman clear of her torture chamber. Wentworth fell, tumbled down the steep slope of the deck, brought up stunningly against a stanchion. Life-preservers! He reeled to his feet. The rack was empty, and there was no time to look. Under his feet, the boat seemed to be moving forward with gathering speed. God, she was diving to the bottom! Suction would drag down anyone too near. Even those on his slowly drifting plane might not be safe.

Wentworth caught the woman's unconscious body into his arms, toed the rail and leaped wide into the sea. For an instant, his head bobbed clear of the surface, then the water clutched at him with a hundred irresistible hands, dragging him down—down. He clasped a palm over the woman's mouth and nostrils, lashed out with his feet against the suction. The pressure of immense depths hammered at his ears. His lungs strained to bursting, but he dared not relieve them even by expelling air. It would end his buoyancy of body. The brawling, whirling water yanked savagely at the woman in his arms. Blackness... But even in numb half-unconsciousness, Wentworth held tightly to the woman and fought, fought....

It was when hope had left him that, amazingly, he found his head above water, felt the grateful rush of air into his lungs. Weakness loosened his muscles, but feebly he rolled to his back, supporting the woman's head on his chest. Presently, he could look about again. Low in the air above the water was a pall of black smoke, a ghost of steam. The surface was scattered with wreckage, floating chairs, shattered ends of railings. Near him floated a woman in a life-preserver. Her head sagged and tears rolled down her cheeks. She made no sound at all. There were others that screamed and fought and, even while he watched, three heads vanished from the surface. But he could do nothing....

The thrashing roar of plane engines pierced his consciousness, and he saw them taxiing among the wreckage. Men were picking up the survivors. He had been wrong, then, about them being the Whisper's men. Thank God for so much. Feebly, Wentworth stroked toward the nearest. If they could take care of the woman! And then he heard the sharp burst of gunfire and men's distant shouts! More deaths to add to this horror. Heaven grant that it was the death of the Whisper's men that he heard. Then, deliberately, came three spaced shots.

On the plane nearest him, Wentworth caught a fleeting glimpse of a man's face—a Chinese! At the sound of that obvious signal, he deliberately pushed overboard a woman he had drawn to the pontoon of his ship! She sank without a struggle. With a bitter oath, Wentworth realized the trickery. These ships were the escape planes of the Whisper. They had made a pretense of rescue until they were needed. And now... the Chinese was moving toward a child in a life-preserver who clung to a pontoon strut. He lifted his foot to kick the child loose.

Wentworth's hand ducked to his armpit. The woman he carried sagged beneath the water, but he tugged his automatic loose. It might work... He squeezed the trigger, and the recoil slammed comfortingly against his wrist muscles. The Chinese turned a startled, bewildered face and pitched backward, threshing, into the water. From the cockpit, a gun blasted back at Wentworth, but his head made a small target. Deliberately, he fired again and saw the pilot wrenched violently backward by his lead—and vanish within the fuselage.

Strong with his rage, Wentworth stroked toward the ship, the unconscious woman in tow. He began the task of getting her and the child into the cockpit. There was no more shooting off toward the *Britannie,* but there were screams, amid the thickness of the clinging smoke, that told him what was happening on the other planes he had seen. Fury was in his soul. He got the woman into the cockpit, tumbled the dead pilot into the sea, reached down for the child.

The child was smiling. "You found Mama!" he cried, and patted the woman's unconscious face. "You found Mama!" To the sound of that baby voice, the woman responded with some dim and struggling spark of life. She stirred, and her eyelids fluttered.

"Thank you, man," said the child.

WENTWORTH GAZED at them helplessly. How could he fly into battle with them? But there were other planes nearby. If he could seize another... Savagely Wentworth wrenched at the throttle of the ship, kicked the rudder bar, groping in near-darkness for the enemy. He found one at last and his guns hammered out his challenge. Lead slammed into the fuselage near him. A glass splinter slashed at his cheek, but he got the two men in the other plane, plunged into the water to swim to it—and realized that there were a dozen helpless people floundering around him, drifting. The boats would come soon and save them—had to save them. Over there, the Whisper was escaping! Wentworth climbed up on the pontoon of the second ship, and he heard a woman sob, the cry of a child. Wentworth knotted his fists in despair. He couldn't go—not while these unfortunates needed his help.

"This way!" he called. "Paddle this way. Here are two planes. They'll hold a lot of people... until the boats come."

He heard the roaring of plane motors, as the ships took off, The Whisper's men were fleeing to safety with their loot, escaping while their prey, who were no more than bait for a ruthlessly inhuman trap, still struggled in the water. Still, he labored on. It seemed hours before the splash and rasping of oars nearby heralded a boat, other hours before he could transfer those he had rescued to that safety. But when he straightened he could still hear, faintly, the beat of the plane motors.

Exultantly, he leaped to the cockpit of the ship, palmed the compression starter button. He chafed at the necessity of taxiing very slowly at first—both for fear of running down human beings and of puncturing the pontoons on wreckage. Finally, he thrust clear and yanked the throttle wide. At last the Spider could take the vengeance trail!

CHAPTER 9
VENGEANCE FROM THE SKY

WENTWORTH WAS not flying wholly blind. He had marked well the direction most of the planes had seemed to take and he hurled his captured ship into the northeast. He had hoped to find some directions on the bodies of the men he had slain—perhaps a clue to the leader who claimed their allegiance. But that had been vain. As he rose in a long slant, he peered back and saw the questing searchlights, the myriad flares that marked the rescue work. How many scores had perished back there? The full toll might never be known. The channel tides were swift....

Wentworth settled to the job that lay before him, began to examine the ship. There were no machine guns, but he had plenty of small arms—his own and those of the two killers. If only he could locate the rendezvous, there was a chance he might trap and slay the Whisper. He flew one of the man's own ships. It was not too much to hope that, in the confusion of the

get-away, he might get close enough to use his guns! If he could find that rendezvous....

Confound it, there must be something here that would tell him the course! These men certainly were not very familiar with the territory. To his certain knowledge, there were not a

CITY OF WHISPERING DEATH

The sleek craft was enveloped in flames from the dumped gasoline!

half-dozen Chinese pilots around New York. He knew them all and they were fine chaps. They would have nothing to do with such killing scum as these. Yet the Whisper's men, strangers to the coast, were expected to find a rendezvous in the darkness, without even the aid of a chart. There was a radio receiver—no sending equipment—but his listening ears discovered nothing on the air waves that might be a guide. Could the instrument board...? He frowned, puzzling.

Abruptly, Wentworth uttered a low cry. The plane was equipped with an earth induction compass—the type that could be set for a prescribed course. It registered, not north and south like an ordinary magnetic compass, but variations from the course for which it was set. Wentworth laughed softly. It was as simple as that! He swung the plane in a slow turn until the needle of the compass hovered at zero, held her nose there. One thing was certain. The ships could not land in darkness—there was no equipment for blind flying or landing—and if he held his course he must ultimately spot their flares or floods.

The black water beneath him gave place to the scattered lights of Long Island. Impatiently, he speeded the ship. There could be no landing here for sea-planes. It must be the North Shore then.

Time was leaden, but finally the lights were dropping behind again. Wentworth twisted impatiently in his seat. His eyes ached from long straining at the darkness ahead. Confound it, the landing must be somewhere now! This course, after Long Island fell behind, would not touch land again until he struck the jutting peninsula of Nova Scotia. The Whisper would never get so far from his base of operations in New York!

Was it possible that, after all, Wentworth had misread the meaning of the induction compass?

Perhaps he was supposed to fly to left or right of the exact course, and… It was then he spotted the flares. If his attention had not been focused so sharply on his exact course, he must have seen them before—twenty miles to his right. A shadow, that was a landing plane, swooped between him and the flare, then another. Wentworth's lips set in harsh determination and deliberately he swung toward the spot. It would take him less than ten minutes. They could not all escape in that time.

Steadily, Wentworth's hand lifted to his guns. He gripped the stick between his knees, made certain his weapons were ready. The flare blacked out, but Wentworth needed it no longer. A few minutes later, he swung in a wide circle over a land-locked cove and, from below, a broad-beamed searchlight reached out and bathed the ship. Wentworth yanked on the red release lever of a flare—and the right edge of the cockpit, just beside his shoulder suddenly became a mass of bullet-torn splinters!

INSTINCTIVELY, WENTWORTH kicked the rudder. He felt the jarring hammer of machine-gun bullets tear up through the fuselage behind him. He gunned the idling motor, swept in a tight *virage* toward the shelter of darkness. The searchlight still pinned him against the velvet sky, but dimly he could make out the flicker of three machine guns, set in a triangle about that light. The devil! He knew what that meant. As long as the light was on him, those machine guns would have his range! How had he betrayed himself—by coming in from the wrong direction? Perhaps, he should have answered that questing beam of light with some signal. That must be it....

Anger shook Wentworth. Was he to be cheated of his prey at the last moment? He wrenched the ship about, saw bullet-holes spatter the right wing like dark drops of blood. He was not yet beaten! From an altitude of a thousand feet, he threw the plane into a slashing power-dive—straight into the beam of the searchlight! It seemed a mad thing to do, but Wentworth's genius for attack had shown him the way. The heavy motor before him formed a bulletproof shield for his body, as long as he kept the nose true on the light. He'd see if they had the courage to await his charge!

As the wind screamed with mounting momentum, Wentworth cut his motor and his hand stole to the dump-valve of the gasoline tank. A grim smile was on his lips. He could hear the raving stammer of the machine guns and the screaming of the steel slicing the air so close above his head. The motor rang to a hail of bullets and the punctured propeller, in dying revolutions, made an eerie siren whine. Less than two hundred feet to dive and his speed was mounting every moment.

As the ship covered the last few score of feet, Wentworth yanked the dump-valve, immediately jerking the lever that released his second landing flare. The stick came back and the centrifugal force of that violent leveling sagged him deep into his seat, blotted out his sight as it drained the blood from his brain. In those numb, blind instants that followed, Wentworth's reflexes flew for him as he had set them to do. He had made worse pull-outs than this. Test pilots had to throw their ships into a 9 G turn, and you couldn't attain anything like that with a thousand-foot dive.

In a moment, Wentworth's full senses returned to him. He was zooming at a steep angle from momentum, his motor dead, undoubtedly pierced in a dozen vital places by bullets. He put the nose down and, for the first time, could look back. He had missed the blast in his momentary black-out, but he could now see the success of his attack. The deluging gasoline had been set off by the flare. Angry red flames were boiling upward from a low-lying rakish boat which mounted the machine guns and light. In the lurid glare, he could see men darting about, black silhouettes. Beyond them, a dozen planes floated upon the cove.

Harsh laughter twisted Wentworth's lips. He hoped some had had the courage to stick by those guns! If they had, they would die now as terribly as some had died aboard the excursion boat! But his ship was rapidly losing altitude. He made a careful turn and slanted toward a dead-stick landing on the cove! He could hear the shouting of the men above the roar of the fire, the popping of pistols—see their angry red stabs of flame. They might hit him. It was a chance he must run—no dodging in a motorless ship.

He leveled cautiously in the ample light of the flames. He was not through with his mission of destruction. The Whisper might have counted on the boat for escape, but planes were useful, too. By careful manipulation, Wentworth thought he might manage to wreck three of them in landing!

HIS SKIDS snagged the surface of the water and Wentworth threw the plane sideways. His left wing sliced into that of a stationary ship. Both crumpled. The impact whirled the landing plane violently. Wentworth was thrown to his knees, but his floating Juggernaut glided on and its shattered nose rammed another of the Whisper's craft. There was a clatter of metal striking, grinding—and another ship was out of commission with a damaged propeller!

Instantly, Wentworth was up and swarming over the edge of the cockpit. Guns *whanged* from all directions. It was clear that not all of the men had reached land from their planes. Other men ran along the shore, firing. Wentworth shouted his challenge and hit the water in a clean dive. He had chosen his goal before he leaped, and he stroked beneath the surface with frantic speed. The nearest plane was sixty feet away, within easy reach for an expert swimmer like Wentworth. Presently he rolled to his back and, nearing the surface, watched for the black shadow of the plane above him.

When finally he came up, it was beneath the craft's wings. There were men in it. He could hear their shouts, but their dialect of Chinese was strange to him. Noiselessly, he clambered up on the inner side of one of the pontoons, but he neglected to consider the delicate balance of the ship. A face jutted over the side of the cockpit, a gun reached toward him… Wentworth's draw and pull on the trigger were lightning fast, and his gun missed fire! The man laughed, took deliberate aim.

Wentworth threw his gun, but it was a quick toss without much force behind it. The Chinese fired, but he had flinched and Wentworth dropped safely into the water. Men were wading after him now. Beneath the surface, Wentworth heard the pulse of a small motor. But he did not attempt to dodge away. If he could capture this plane, he would be master of the situation again. Surely the forces of the law must come soon. The sound of the shots would carry far through the night and the flaring fire aboard the boat would attract attention. If he could hold the Whisper and his men here....

Wentworth ducked under the pontoon to the opposite side of the ship and once more crawled from the surface. He clenched a gun, reversed in his hand, as he scrambled upon the wing. Men were shouting, firing at him. Warnings cried to the gunman in the cockpit. As he lifted, Wentworth saw the man's moon-yellow face turn toward him, heard his shriek as he swiveled his gun. No time to cover the distance between them. Once more, Wentworth threw a gun and this time with the entire strength of his shoulder behind it.

The gun crashed into the man's face, the instant he fired. He was wrenched violently backward over the side of the cockpit, and Wentworth was on him. His strangle hold was unnecessary. The man was dead, the entire front of his skull caved in. Wentworth took his gun, tumbled him overboard and made a lightning-swift survey of the cove by the dying light of the gasoline blaze.

The small boat he had heard—an outboard motor skiff—was still a hundred yards away. Even as he stared at it, a man stood up in its prow and a submachine gun began to pour lead toward him. His captured revolver would have no accuracy at that distance. Wentworth dropped into the pilot's seat and jammed in the starter button. It whined—the motor caught with a roar. He kicked the rudder, started the plane in a sweeping turn. He could easily distance the outboard motor, wreck the other planes. Triumph welled up in Wentworth's breast. Perhaps he had succeeded, after all, in trapping the Whisper! Perhaps, finally—

Then a frown dented his forehead. Something was wrong with the way the ship handled. It persisted in wrenching toward the right. The wing on that side was a little low... With a curse, Wentworth understood. That Chinese bullet, that had missed him, had punctured the pontoon. It was leaking badly, would sink him before he could work the damage he planned. Only one thing to do—seize another ship, or....

He glanced about him. From three near-by planes, bullets screamed toward him The motor-boat... He glanced over his shoulder. He had not managed to widen the distance, and the submachine gun bursts were reaching toward him. Violently, Wentworth wrenched the throttle wide, held the rudder hard over while his plane gathered speed.

IT WAS a frantic eternity before the plane lifted to the step and he could ease the pressure of the rudder. The ship took off drunkenly, wobbling, just as it was clearing the cove—and a cross-wind from behind the headlands struck him. The ship staggered, stubbed its pontoons in a low wave. The waterlogged weight of the pontoon did its work. Wentworth felt it tilt that way and, as the wing dug into the surface, he freed himself. The next instant he was whirling through the air.

Even then, Wentworth did not lose his presence of mind. Acrobatics, like every other branch of athletic endeavor, were part of the rigid training to which Wentworth had given himself. He balled, then straightened out of his somersaulting with arms flung above his head. He struck the water like a lance, feet first, body in a perfect line. Even so, the shock of the landing was severe. The hard blow of the water jarred through him and he plunged down… down into the coldness of crushing depths.

The chill served to counteract the shock and, only seconds later, he was stroking powerfully toward the surface. He bobbed up long enough to snatch a breath, then submerged noiselessly and swam on. His drenched clothing weighed enormously. Shoes were like anchors on his feet, and the numbness of fatigue began to do its work. When, finally, he could touch bottom and stand with his head just above water to breathe, he was near exhaustion. He stared wearily around. The plane had sunk already and the boat turned back into the cove. He dragged himself to shore, sagged full-length on the sand to rest and plan….

The cove was a full half-mile away across the headland, and he was without weapons. But he would not give up the battle. He drove himself to his feet, struggled through deep sand that trapped his every step. An eternity passed while he crossed that headland and, before he could once more spot the cove through the thick-growing scrub trees, firelight licked toward the sky. Wentworth swore and began to run. Were they destroying their own planes? That meant they had another means of escape—automobiles, perhaps!

Wentworth's breath labored noisily from his throat. He staggered and twice fell, as he fought his way on toward the cove. A booming explosion sent sparks and flame soaring into the air and he felt the thud of the concussion. But there was another sound in the night sky now, the distant hum of airplane motors. Wentworth almost sobbed with relief. Other planes on hand could mean only that pursuit had at last run down the fugitive hideout. But it was too late unless he could signal the pilots, and the alarm could be flashed over Long Island, roads closed....

Wentworth burst out on the shore of the cove. Every plane was ablaze. The boat was a fire-shattered hulk above which the skeleton of the searchlight and guns stood out blackly. How would he signal the planes? Wentworth ran out on the beach, jerked off his coat and ripped it in two up the back seam. He could semaphore. Surely these would be police or army planes— perhaps a coast-guard patrol. Any of them would understand his code.

The ship swung overhead, and Wentworth whirled the parts of his coat for attention, began his message. *"Britannie pirates fleeing by auto. Men Chinese. Notify police."*

The plane swung once more, then skittered down on the surface of the cove close ashore. Wentworth ran toward it.

"Don't take time to land!" he shouted. "Get that message to the police!"

The man climbed out of the pilot's cockpit and sprang into the shallow water, waded ashore.

"You fool!" Wentworth shouted. "If we close the roads, there's time. If we don't...."

The man lifted his goggles and, with the same gesture, whipped out an automatic.

"Police have already closed the roads, Wentworth," he said coldly. "But you and I have a score to settle. You murdered a friend of mine—Delehanty Louis. I've been looking for you ever since you stole that plane this afternoon."

Wentworth swore raggedly, recognizing the man as the soldier-of-fortune who had sworn to run him down, Martin Meggs.

"Don't be a fool," Wentworth said shortly. "If you kill me, you'll be executed. This isn't Spain."

Meggs smiled slowly. "No, it isn't Spain. But I have a deputy sheriff's badge. You're a fugitive from justice, and it's easy enough to say you resisted arrest."

Wentworth started forward, but the gun centered on his body unwaveringly. He saw that Megg's eyes were steady, implacable.

"I'll give you precisely the same chance you gave my friend," said Meggs softly. "I've got a gun in my hand. You've got one in your holster. Draw it, quickly—I'm not a patient man. Go on—quick!"

CHAPTER 10
CHALLENGE AT MIDNIGHT

WENTWORTH TOLD Meggs impatiently that he didn't have a gun, and the man smiled his incredulity. Wentworth lifted his arms and the empty holsters showed plainly.

"Go ahead and shoot," he said harshly. "From what I've heard of you modern soldiers-of-fortune, a little thing like shooting down an unarmed man wouldn't trouble you."

Martin Meggs' eyes glinted in the lurid light, but with what emotion Wentworth was unable to say. His dragging weariness still gripped him and, for once, his keen brain seemed unable to find a way out of his dilemma. One thing, he knew. It was death that looked at him out of this man's eyes. It was not mercy that stayed his hand even for these few moments. Meggs was *enjoying* his plight.

Desperately, in his need, Wentworth's eyes quested about him. There was no cover nearer than deep water and he stood no chance at all of reaching it before a half-dozen bullets tore through his body. There was a fragment of rotten branch, a yard from his left foot, but it was useless as a weapon, unless... Wentworth smiled slightly.

"If you insist that I arm myself before you shoot," he said dryly, "I'll pick up that piece of wood and you can pretend, in the darkness, that you thought it was a gun."

As he spoke, he took the half-step necessary to pick it up, bent far over toward it. Meggs watched him with his glinting eyes, gun ready, saying nothing. It was only natural that his eyes should watch the left hand reach for the stick.

Wentworth had called it a weapon. It was plain that Meggs expected it to be thrown at him and was more than ready. But that hard concentration was just what Wentworth had hoped for. His right hand slid inconspicuously down his side and, while his left still reached for the stick, he flung a clutched handful of sand full and hard into Meggs' face! In the same movement, he took a long leap past the stick in the direction he leaned.

The gun blasted, deafeningly. Wentworth felt a burning shock run across his shoulders. It drove him half to his knees as he scooped up another double handful of sand and flung it. Meggs was swearing in a thin, vicious voice, digging at his eyes with his left hand, trying to sight clearly. The gun hammered again, but Wentworth went in under it, feet-first, in a base runner's slide. His heels drove Meggs' ankles out from under him. His hands shot up and seized Meggs' gun-wrist and, holding on savagely, he threw his entire weight into a roll to the right.

Meggs was already pitching forward. His right arm was twisted, straightened and levered up almost to the breaking point. He fell on his face and Wentworth, his roll completed, had that arm in a cruel *jiu-jitsu* grip. His left armpit, all his body's weight, was over Meggs' biceps and elbow, his two hands strained upward on the stiffened arm. With a muffled curse, Meggs released the gun. Wentworth changed his grip, got agilely to his knees.

"What action," Wentworth asked mockingly, "do the rules and by-laws of soldiers-of-fortune suggest now?"

Meggs swore at him bitterly, but with difficulty because of the pressure that held his face against the sand. Wentworth laughed, struck with hooked taut fingers just beneath the ear and Meggs went limp after a convulsive jerk. That same blow, delivered with sufficient force, would kill, but Wentworth had no intention of injuring Meggs. He had struck purely in self-defense. Whatever the man's conceit, Wentworth could not quarrel with the motive of personal revenge for a friend.

He arose, scooped up Meggs' gun and strode rapidly toward where the plane was lightly grounded in the shallows, waded out and, a few minutes later, spun it for a take-off. As he lifted from the water, Meggs staggered to his feet on the sand and Wentworth swung a mocking hand to him. Slowly, Wentworth's momentary exultation faded. Whatever he might think of Meggs, the man had been a deadly peril there on the sands. There had been no question of his will and intent to kill. There must be no more carelessness such as this. The Spider's life was too valuable to the cause he served. Grimness settled upon his features, as he turned the plane's nose toward New York City.

TO HIS left lay the myriad tangled highways of Long Island. How quickly had the roads been blockaded, he wondered, and how thoroughly? The very fact that the Whisper had chosen flight to Long Island argued that he had his retreat fully mapped. It was true that he might have expected to use boat or planes, but a man who would think to arrange a landing signal—even for his own planes—against the possibility of capture and pursuit, would have surely provided for that contingency. If only Wentworth had been able to maintain contact!

Search of the roads was a task the police could perform better than Wentworth, but there was plenty of work for the Spider in New York. His hand moved swiftly to the radio dials, and he picked up a news broadcast. The announcer was just concluding an account of the wreck of the *S. S. Happiness.*

"This is the culmination of a reign of terror that has had all

New York by the throat," he pounded on, staccato-voiced. "It is the worst outbreak, but it is by no means all. Tonight, in New York, Deputy District Attorney Carmichael was cut down by the mysterious whispering death as he left his office to go home. At the same time, police admitted reluctantly that five complainants in racket cases, on which the new city administration was depending to smash the grip of the Underworld upon the city, have completely disappeared. The police do not deny that they believe these five persons to have been kidnaped!"

Wentworth swore softly and his hand knotted on the stick, until the knuckles were white. Not content with his savage looting of the *Britannie,* the Whisper had been busy with his terrorization in New York. Five kidnappings and a murder! The Underworld would soon launch a veritable *jihad* against the people if this sort of thing continued. It might already be too late to avert the fearful crime wave that surely would follow such a shattering of the forces of law and order.

Only one thing might still avert it—the Spider must institute his own reign of terror and wipe out the big shots, one by one. The Underworld must come to regard him with the same superstitious dread that they now felt for the Whisper. The way in which this could be done was simple, but incredibly dangerous—especially for a man whom police, as well as Underworld, hunted. He must challenge his victims, appoint time and place, then strike successfully despite the guards with which the man would ring him round, despite watchful police—and the Whisper himself! Wentworth smiled bitterly. Probably, Martin Meggs would be on hand for his revenge as well!

Mike Casaroma came first. If the Spider challenged, Casaroma would not dare to decline lest his own men believe him afraid. Such men as Casaroma dominate solely by a personal hold upon their men; and it was easy for morale to be shattered once they believed him afraid. There were even more powerful reasons. Casaroma and the Whisper would welcome a chance to trap the Spider and kill him. Well, he would give them the chance. He would kill Casaroma, and he prayed that the Whisper would also come to the scene! But he thought he could count on that. Kill Casaroma, follow the Whisper, free Nita and the other prisoners, provided the Spider, himself, was not killed!

Throughout the flight back, Wentworth laid plans. When he landed the plane off a deserted East River dock, he was ready. He found a deflated rubber boat on the sea-plane, as he had hoped, made a compact bundle of it and vanished into the city toward the hideout of Blinky McQuade. He must rest for a while, recoup his strength for the battle ahead.

It was a half-hour later that a newspaper man received a phone call and heard a mocking, flat voice that he knew. Afterward, the newspaper office went wild and the extras flooded again to the streets, headlines screaming—

SPIDER CHALLENGES CASAROMA
RACKET CHIEF ACCEPTS DUEL IN CENTRAL PK.
DENIES SPIDER'S CHARGES HE WAS RESPON-
SIBLE FOR *BRITANNIE* DISASTER

CASAROMA CALLS IT 'DUTY'
"I'M AN HONEST CITIZEN," HE SAYS, "AND WILL

BE GLAD TO DO THIS SERVICE FOR CITY"

The police moved swiftly. Central Park was closed to traffic, to pedestrians. Commissioner Kirkpatrick gave out a statement that the police had not been asked to protect Casaroma; that duels were against the law and that both participants, or the survivor, would be tried for murder. Aside from that, he said that the Spider already was wanted for murder and that the police would make every effort to arrest him before the affair took place.

AS MIDNIGHT approached, Fifth Avenue and Central Park West were thick with people, windows jammed. At the spot the Spider had designated—the east bank of the lake near Eighty-Sixth Street along the western drive—Casaroma stood alone. But within twenty feet of him were a half-dozen armed bodyguards and, beyond them, surrounding the lake, blocking the walks, pacing sentry-go along the ridges, were several hundred police. Kirkpatrick had his headquarters on a knoll a hundred feet away and, in the bright moonlight, could see clearly down to the lake shores. One of his deputies was with him.

"The Spider—Wentworth, or whoever he is—won't ever make it," the man said. "It's just a bluff. At best, he'll use a rifle from some rooftop."

Kirkpatrick's face was set and grim. "I don't share your optimism," he said flatly. "The Spider told the newspapers he would appear in person, meet Casaroma face to face and that Casaroma should have an equal chance. The Spider, whatever his sin—and God knows they are many—will keep his word."

On the bank of the lake, Casaroma walked back and forth

with a strut. It was two minutes of midnight. He carried a revolver in his right hand, and his men watched him admiringly. It took nerve to accept a challenge like that from the Spider. They were contemptuous of the police. Hell, the Whisper tied them in knots!

Casaroma stopped and peered suspiciously into the depths of the lake, turned and stared at the shrub-thick knolls around. The air was heavy, motionless, and carried his harsh oath even to Kirkpatrick's ears.

"Come on out, Spider!" Casaroma called. "I'm ready and waiting for you! Are you yellow?"

There was no answer, and the raucous laughter of the waiting gunmen drifted out across the lake. Off in the distance, a deep-toned bell began to ring. Casaroma stood rigidly waiting on the shores of the lake and, as the strokes rang on, police stopped their pacing of sentry duty counting the strokes. They were slow, portentous. When they had reached ten, Casaroma threw back his head and laughed again.

"I told you!" he shouted. "I told you the Spider was afraid. It's midnight and he ain't here!"

The eleventh and twelfth strokes boomed out, slowly.

"Afraid!" Casaroma shouted. "You're afraid, Spider!"

He had his back turned toward the lake. That was why he did not see the first gentle ripple and the slow rising of a man's head close in shore. His men saw the black-caped and hatted figure of the Spider rise from the shallows and shouted, but it was the Spider's voice that spun Casaroma about to face him.

"Afraid of you, Casaroma?" said the Spider softly, "Afraid of you?" And the Spider laughed—a flat, hard, mocking sound as he strode straight from the shallows. His hands were empty!

With a hoarse shout, Casaroma flung up his gun and squeezed the trigger. The bullet plucked into the water, went ricocheting across toward the far bank. He was shaking with terror and superstitious dread of this awesome nemesis who could rise thus from the black water. He tried to shoot again, but there was no time. In a long bound, the Spider had him. A wrench flung the gun from his hand, then the Spider's arms locked about his body, lifted him—and the Spider backed out again into the depths of the lake!

"Casaroma must drown," Wentworth's deep voice belled through the night, "to pay for those others who died when the *Happiness* went down!" That was all.

Casaroma squealed like a frightened rabbit. He struggled and beat with hands and feet. His men were racing toward him. Across the lake, police shouted challenges and rushed to the shore, but they could not shoot. No man could have seen clearly enough to tell which of those two struggling figures was the Spider and which was Casaroma....

WENTWORTH HAD moved swiftly, taking advantage of that first wild surprise to reach Casaroma. After that, he knew there would be no danger of shooting from other sources, and he had disarmed Casaroma. Before the man's paralysis of terror deserted him, Wentworth turned and heaved Casaroma from him into deeper water, sucked in a deep breath and dived beneath the surface. Seconds later, his hands closed on Casaroma's threshing feet and dragged him down. The lake was twelve feet deep in the middle, and Wentworth had hooked weights to his belt. He went straight to the bottom with his prey.

Casaroma fought wildly. His flailing arms struck blindly, and a blow across Wentworth's face drove his head violently back. Wentworth felt a sharp pain in his cheek and realized that Casaroma wielded a knife! Wentworth seized the man's wrist and struck out with his fist. He felt it jar, but the water impeded him. There was little force to it. His lungs strained and there was a pounding fury in his temples. He would have to go up for air. It would not be easy with the heavy weights about his waist and Casaroma's knife....

With darkness gathering in his brain, to match the impenetrable blackness of the muddy, roiled water, Wentworth loosened the belt which bound the weights about his waist. Still gripping Casaroma's knife wrist, he thrust violently toward the surface. Casaroma's struggles were weaker, enfeebled by the same need for air, but Wentworth's mouth was set in a relentless line. These were the agonies through which the poor creatures on the *Happiness* had passed. It was just that Casaroma should suffer so!

Wentworth expelled air as he neared the surface. His head burst out. Instantly, he had filled his lungs and was diving again. He heard a bedlam of shouts. A single gun had blasted in that brief moment. Casaroma was fighting furiously, and there were no weights to help Wentworth drag him down this time. The knife broke from his grasp. With a lunge and a dive, Wentworth tried to circle Casaroma and catch him from behind.

He had fastened the guide rope which he had tied to his own ankle so that he could return to his hiding place when the struggle was over. It caught on some obstruction, jerked him violently, and he felt a blow on his shoulder, a hand seize his throat! Wentworth ignored the strangle hold. Impossible to breathe below the surface anyway. With both hands, he seized the arm that had struck his shoulder.

Casaroma's strength was incredible. The man was undoubtedly in the throes of drowning, and desperation lent him fury. With a single twist, he wrenched his knife hand free and high. Wentworth knew that it was coming down. Impossible to tear loose from that strangle hold and dodge. Equally impossible to see the falling blow. One thing was in his favor. The stab would come slowly because of the water that impeded their every movement. Wentworth knew once more the doomed ringing of suffocation in his ears. How Casaroma still could fight on he did not know, for Wentworth had managed to catch but one fresh breath of air. Casaroma had had none.

Wentworth realized that his own movements were slowing, and that deadly knife… Desperately, Wentworth doubled up his legs and struck out violently with both feet. He felt them strike home. The grip on his throat was released… but Casaroma was free! Free or not, Wentworth knew that he had to breathe. He stroked for the surface, snatched his breath of grateful air, and dived again. He did not see Casaroma rise. Had that kick done the trick? Wentworth stroked through the black depths, feeling before him with groping hands.

Death well might wait for him here—death on the slashing knife of Casaroma—but death equally was there on the surface. The instant he was recognized, a dozen guns would pour their deadly lead into him. Abruptly, his shoulder drove against an obstruction that yielded softly and surged away from him. He seized it, groped for the knife hand, but there was no resistance—none at all. And Wentworth's fumbling hands felt the hilt of the knife—*protruding from Casaroma's side!*

SUICIDE TO stop the awful terror of drowning? Or had Wentworth's kick driven the blade into its owner's body? No one would ever know now. It did not matter. From Wentworth's pocket, he ripped a newspaper whose pictures of that horror at sea had tortured him. He jammed it over the knife handle, lifted Casaroma's body over his head. The movement shoved Wentworth to the bottom and, as his feet touched, he threw his strength into an upward heave.

Casaroma's body had some small buoyancy left. At least it would bob to the surface, no matter how soon it sank thereafter. Wentworth wanted Casaroma's fellows to see and know that he had paid for his crimes! But the Spider would have to move swiftly now. No way of telling how soon his hiding place would be found, and the time was fast approaching when he must catch another breath.

All his movements were leaden, heavy with fatigue. Those inadequate gasps of air at the surface were far from enough for his oxygen-starved body. He had to grope twice before he could find the rope bound to his own ankle. Once it was in his hands, he moved swiftly. He hauled in on it, hand over hand, his legs streamed out behind him. He shot through the water more rapidly than any stroke could have moved him. Luckily, he had not far to go. His hiding place was no more than twenty feet from the spot where he had walked from the water to attack Casaroma.

Seconds later, his outstretched hand felt the slimy rocks. But he fought against the urge to bound to the surface to breathe. Instead, he let his head break the surface, gently. There he hung through long minutes while his breathing slowed to normal. He could hear the shouts of searching men all around, but it would take a strong light and a keen-eyed man to reveal his hiding place. Here the rocky bank of the lake dropped almost cliff-like to the water, and there were rock fragments that jutted above the surface. Upon them, Wentworth had rested a shell of inflated rubber, taken from the rubber boat off Meggs' plane, and painted to match the background. He had been here within a half-hour after calling the newspaper.

Yes, the entrance had been easy enough, but his escape was going to be more difficult. It had been impossible to arrange anything for that. He knew there would be dozens of police cars about, and he was counting on reaching one of those.

A new note had entered the shouting and hunt-cries around him.

"There's a body!" a man yelled. "Look—*it's Casaroma!*"

And, not far away, Kirkpatrick's crisp voice. "Bring those searchlights right down to the edge of the water. They'll light up the lake, as soon as that mud settles. I don't think the Spider is down there, but we'll soon find out. Throw a tight cordon around the lake, Sergeant."

Wentworth's lips twitched. Yes, it was time to hurry, if Kirkpatrick was in charge. At any moment, his eyes might detect the lack of reflection from the water where the rubber float was lodged. Swiftly, he freed his ankle from the rope, divested himself of his cape and ducked out from under the air pocket beneath the float. He was a black shadow, drifting up the black face of the rock—not a thing a man would notice when his attention was on the cruelly dead Casaroma.

WENTWORTH REACHED the top of the fifteen-foot embankment and was among thick shrubs. Fifty feet away were four police cars… but moving directly toward him was a policeman with a flashlight. Behind him, Kirkpatrick's voice rang out, crisply.

"Over there by the rocks, there's a dark spot that will bear investigation."

"Just a rock, Commissioner," a man answered.

"Investigate!" Kirkpatrick snapped. "Rocks don't move up and down with the waves!" His voice lifted. "Is there a man on top that knoll?"

The policeman with the flashlight turned aside a little from Wentworth, mounted a stump.

"Here, Commissioner!" he called.

"Keep your eyes open!" Kirkpatrick called back. "We've spotted his hiding place!"

Wentworth gathered his legs beneath him and, as the policeman stepped down, he sprang forward. The man's cry started in his throat, then Wentworth's fist connected with his jaw. Faint as it was, Kirkpatrick's watchful attention caught it.

"Quickly!" he cried. "Up on that knoll! The sentry has been attacked!"

There was no smile on Wentworth's lips now. There was no man in the world he would rather have working beside him than Kirkpatrick and, by the same token, there could be no keener foe. He was sprinting for the parked police cars in the same instant his blow went home against the policeman's jaw. If there was a guard there, he was finished.

But he was sure that the man he had felled had been on watch at the parking place. He knew, too, the carelessness with which police left their keys in their cars.

Wentworth darted to the first car—and found the key gone. He raced to the second, the third, and a gasp of relief gusted from him. He sprang to the wheel of the coupé, kicked the starter. From the crest of the knoll, a revolver crashed out and a hole starred through the windshield—but Wentworth had the machine rolling now. They would be after him full cry, but the keys were gone from the other cars as he had reason to know. And the owners were unlikely to be the first to reach them. In a police car, he could crash the exits of the park. Once outside, he was safe.

He threw a glance into the rear-vision mirror, and his blood ran cold in his veins. Wentworth was not a man to whom fear came readily, but the sight of the thing in the rumble seat would have made a weaker man scream aloud. The rumble-seat cover had lifted and, peering at him, through the rear window of the coupé, was the devil mask of the Whisper. A cross-bow was aimed at Wentworth through that window... a cross-bow whose missile would flick through that glass as if it had been cheese-cloth—and cut off his head with the same facility.

CHAPTER 11
CITY OF FEAR

WENTWORTH DID a thing then that would have been impossible for most men. He drove calmly on, removing his eyes off that dread death-mask behind him before the Whisper could become aware that he was discovered. At any second, that fearful, slashing weapon might be fired at him. If he made any move to draw a gun—to execute the awkward twist that would permit him to fire back over his shoulder at the Whisper—he would be instantly killed. Was there no way out? Was the Spider to die thus ignominiously in the very moment of victory? His jaw set firmly.

Only one chance remained to him and that very attempt might cost his life. Not fifty feet ahead was a bridge over one of the cross-cuts that burrowed through the park from east to west. Fifteen feet below was the drive, and it would be closed to traffic by the police guard intended to prevent the Spider's escape. If he dived the car into that… There, was nothing else left for him to do.

He decided.

Careful not to move his shoulders by so much as an inch, Wentworth slid a left hand to the door-catch. He needed to do no more than spring it. The wind would rip it wide. But a leap into space at fifty miles an hour… Wentworth's lips closed rock firm. He sprang the catch, lunged out the door and wrenched the wheel in a single whipping movement of his body. He heard glass crash, then he was plunging through the air. It was if a tornado roared in his ears.

The door, checked for an instant by its stop-strap as it tugged wide in the wind, slammed against Wentworth's thigh. It spun him in a flat-sprawling whirl. He saw thick shrubbery flash toward him. He tried to ball, to take the fall rolling. Jagged ends of branches slashed and tore at him. He struck on left shoulder and hip, tumbled sideways through crashing bushes. His whole side went numb but, with reeling head, he staggered to his feet. Somewhere near—on top of him, it seemed—there sounded a rending crash, a tinny mingling of torn metal and shattering glass; a second, louder concussion, then... silence.

Swaying dizzily on his feet, Wentworth saw the sagging breach in the iron guard rail where the car had crashed through, the rip in the shrubbery where it had plowed through to the verge. He took two reeling steps toward the brink over which the car had plunged and the nausea of shock began to pump at his belly. His head spun. Frantically, he peered about, and a choked laugh blurted from his lips. That trashcan, modeled into the likeness of a tree trunk, would just hold the Spider. He staggered toward it, darkness gathering in his brain, clambered in with fumbling legs... and darkness swept over him.

IT COULD not have been more than a few moments later that consciousness began to come back, but the shouts of men were all around him. He peered out, vision still blurred, and saw a jumble of parked cars and streaming headlights. That lean figure striding toward the edge of the cross-cut was Kirkpatrick.

• *NITA VAN SLOAN* •

He could hear his clipped, crisp voice, but the words didn't seem to make sense. Then, abruptly, the picture slipped into focus.

"There was a man in that rumble seat!" Kirkpatrick shouted. "I saw him just before the turn in the road. A man in a devil-mask and a purple robe—the Whisper! Open that rumble, carefully!"

Wentworth closed his eyes, trying to think. His shoulder and side ached torturingly and there were sharp twinges of pain when he moved it. He could find no broken bones, but he was bleeding from a dozen cuts where rocks or broken branches had stabbed him.

If the Whisper had gone over the edge with the car... Wentworth shook his head. He couldn't possibly have got clear of that rumble seat in time... but if he had crouched low, closed the lid? Yes, that would have done it. Cushions around him, a space too small for a violent blow. He would have been shaken up, but not otherwise injured. Then, the Whisper might still be in the rumble seat! At the thought, Wentworth's hand moved to his gun, then he smiled faintly. There were enough police to take care of that!

A shout from the cross-cut, "It's empty, sir! Here's the robe and mask all right, and a funny sort of bow and arrow. That's all."

Wentworth swore harshly under his breath. Without those distinguishing garments, he, himself, could not recognize the Whisper! The man had made his get-away! And he, himself, was trapped here. Even if he were not found, it might be hours before he could get away. An angry, bawling voice reached his ears.

"That's the inefficiency of the police for you!" It cried. "Two

great criminals in the palm of your hand and you let them escape! I almost trapped Wentworth myself tonight—single-handed!"

Wentworth smiled slightly as he recognized the accents of Martin Meggs. At that, the man had made a quick trip in from Long Island.

"Almost?" Kirkpatrick's tones were sardonic.

"Wentworth is greased lightning," Meggs admitted and told briefly of the happenings at the North Shore cove. "Just a handful of sand against my gun. I could like that man if he hadn't done a low thing like killing Delehanty Louis."

"He seems to have accomplished more than the Long Island police," Kirkpatrick said dryly. "He, at least, ruined their planes. The police couldn't even close the roads, successfully...."

"Commissioner!" a man's voice called harshly. "Mr. Kirkpatrick, sir!"

Wentworth knew those tones, too—Kirkpatrick's official chauffeur.

"There's a report from headquarters, sir," the man raced on. "The dragnet men. They ran into a gun-fight at Second and Bowery. Four of our men are dead. Lieutenant Wilson got killed by the Whispering Death."

Kirkpatrick's voice rasped in a harsh oath. "Get the car," he snapped.

"My God," Meggs whispered. "That's frightful!"

Kirkpatrick did not answer and, peering forth, Wentworth saw him striding rapidly away toward the driveway. Meggs was staring after him and, presently, he moved the same way. Wentworth chafed at his inaction. Damn it, he might as well be locked in a cell as in this damned trashcan, with the police all about! How many hours must elapse before he could slip out? And the men of the Whisper were killing… Wentworth glimpsed Kirkpatrick's activity in that single phrase, 'the drag-net men.' Plainly, Kirkpatrick had ordered a general round-up of all suspicious characters.

Police squads would close in on every known criminal hang-out, arrest men and women on any charge that came to mind—possession of arms, consorting with suspicious characters, violation of parole, vagrancy. Many would be taken directly to railway terminals and sent out of the city. It was a powerful weapon he had loosed against the Underworld, a drastic step. It was true that a great many would be released in courts the next day, but its usual effect was to quiet down the criminal element for days. Strong-arm men would work over the tougher crooks. Fine, if it worked. But the Whisper—and his death-dealing squads—had taken the field! It was open warfare now between the police and all criminals!

WENTWORTH PEERED anxiously about, seeking a way to escape. If Kirkpatrick was going into that kind of battle, he would need the support of the Spider. Already, the Underworld would know of Casaroma's death. If he killed in tandem with the police, spread superstitious dread, it might avert the open anar-chy that threatened. If the police dragnet failed… but it must not fail! Kirkpatrick would understand that. After this defiance, the dragnet must be swept mercilessly through the entire city. If crooks fought back, they must be shot down!

Wentworth grabbed a chance when the space around him

was momentarily clear. The police lines had broken down, and there were many sightseers crowding in despite prohibitions. Newspapermen's cameras were flashing. If he could mingle with them… Moments later, Wentworth managed to slip into a press car and drive rapidly from the park. Police waved him past at the gates—the card in the windshield was effective—and a few blocks away he climbed into his own car and sped southward toward Center Street.

He flicked on the radio, tuned in police signals and heard a muddle of "Signal Thirty" calls. Violence. The radio cars were supplementing the efforts of the dragnet. They cut off abruptly, and Kirkpatrick's crisp, clear voice rang out.

"General orders to call cars, to all raiding squads," he said incisively. "A general round-up of all criminals has been ordered. This must be carried through at all costs. Special riot-guns, grenades and machine guns are being issued. The orders are that, meeting armed resistance, all officers are to shoot to kill! Understand that fully—shoot to kill. Lieutenant Wilson and three men of his squad were murdered by criminals tonight. They can't get away with that, men. Show them what it means to oppose the police. Shoot to kill!"

There was a pause that was electric, then Kirkpatrick finished quietly.

"I am depending on every man to do his full duty. That is all."

Wentworth felt the tension of that message in every fiber of his body and knew that the men who heard it would take a terrible vengeance on the Underworld this night—if they survived.

This was open warfare as New York had never before seen it! If the police faltered, anarchy was at hand!

A block from headquarters, Wentworth parked to wait for Kirkpatrick's exit in the great black limousine that stood, motor running, outside the door. He leaned back against the cushions and tried to relax while he performed such first aid for himself as he could. His left shoulder was stiffening. Obviously, it had been badly sprained in the fall. He examined his various minor wounds, doused them with iodine. He should have a tetanus injection, but that would have to wait. He peered up at his face in the mirror. It was haggard, deeply cut by lines of fatigue and suffering. He closed his eyes. What lay ahead for him this night? Death in any one of a dozen battles, at the hands of police or criminals, was easily possible. Even if the police drive succeeded tonight, that was no end of hostilities. The Whisper must be traced down, his prisoners freed. They would suffer for tonight's attacks, those prisoners! Of one of those prisoners, Wentworth dared not allow himself to think....

Somewhere along the line tonight, he must find the Whisper. If he failed... The Spider pressed a hand, that trembled a little, to his forehead. If he failed, what remained? Abruptly, his head jerked up. In the midst of this mad turmoil of battle, he had overlooked a valuable lead. What was it that Delehanty Louis had cried out before he died? " 'It was blackmail! Either tell where Ada Hamilton was hidden or destroy my own brother!' "

Blackmail! But how could he follow that trail? Certainly, the district attorney would not talk, even if he could be reached. By the heavens, Phyllis Louis, their sister—the girl who had tried to kill him just after Delehanty's death! It was a slim chance, but she might know something in the past lives of Delehanty or his brother that could have been used as a club. She might....

WENTWORTH'S EYES shifted to police headquarters as there came movement at the door. Kirkpatrick strode rapidly toward his car—and two cars squealed around the corner on skidding tires! Even as Wentworth jerked his own machine into motion, a dozen guns opened fire on the commissioner of police!

A fierce shout rose from Wentworth's lips. There was no chance at all that he could get there in time. He had a square to travel to the half-block of the murder-cars, and they were already rolling fast. Wentworth ripped out a gun and fired through the port in his windshield—not with any hope of damaging the assailants, but to distract them for a moment's time.

One of the two men, who had followed Kirkpatrick out the main doors of the headquarters building, was hammered back against the wall by a bullet. He writhed there like a martyr on a cross, twisted and pitched face-down on the top platform. Kirkpatrick was leaping down the steps toward the cover of his parked car, but the assassins were perilously close. Wentworth had the accelerator nailed to the floor and his powerful engine was roaring, but it seemed to him he barely moved. Impossible for Kirkpatrick to escape. A machine gun stammered from the leading car... and Kirkpatrick fell.

It was no fake fall, Wentworth knew instantly. The force of lead had wrenched Kirk about in midair as he leaped down the last steps. He went limp, fell in a crumpled heap on the pavement, fully exposed to the hammer of those guns. White chips of cement flew from the pavement, from the steps. The other policeman was down. A lifetime passed while Wentworth raced down the street after Kirkpatrick fell—a lifetime in thirty seconds.

Then Wentworth sent his car bounding over the curb, slammed on brakes—skidding to a halt squarely between those blazing guns and Kirkpatrick's recumbent body! Instantly, his machine was sieved with pouring lead. His bulletproof windows held for a moment against the pounding of machine-gun bullets, then began to leak jacketed steel slugs. Wentworth had flung wide his door in the instant his car slowed. He flung to the pavement and his two guns were in his hands. A fierce, twisted smile was on his lips—a mask of death itself. His guns jerked and boomed.

Wentworth's hat leaped from his head. A slug creased his sprained left shoulder, but he stood rock-steady!

"You can't kill the Spider!" he cried clearly. "You'll only kill yourselves!"

His first bullet sizzled up the path of the machine gun's fire and its quarter-ton punch hurled the killer violently against the driver of the car. It yawed wildly, and Wentworth turned his guns on the second sedan. His lead spattered frosted spots across the windshield and he cursed flatly at wasted time. Bulletproof, of course. His two guns belched flame together and the right front tire blew out. In the same instant, a bullet found his shoulder and he staggered back, pitched across Kirkpatrick's body.

This was the end!

BLACKNESS SWIRLED in his brain. There was a terrible lethargy in his every movement, but he surged to his feet. He still gripped one gun and only one car was in sight—the second. With its punctured tire, it was jouncing, weaving wildly. It made aiming difficult for the murder men inside, but Wentworth's lead found targets. His right hand lifted under the jerk of his automatic, fell again on a new target, lifted—fell. When he squeezed the trigger, a man died.

He realized another gun was speaking near him, but there was no time to investigate. The gang car, driver dead, turned broadside across the street and jumped the curb. Its nose crushed against the facade of headquarters and bounced. It stood shuddering on its springs like a living, wounded thing, but within it nothing stirred. Wentworth took two heavy steps to his right to peer around the back of his own machine. The other gangster sedan was backing away from a collision with the building opposite. Guns still poured out lead from its rear. Wentworth raised his gun—and from behind him a deafening fusillade crashed out.

Under a deluge of bullets, the back window of the gang car dissolved. Men were driven, broken-backed, across the front seats, riddled, torn apart by lead. Wentworth spun toward Kirkpatrick. The commissioner was braced against the steps. Blood drenched his thigh, but he had a gun in his right hand. For a moment, the eyes of the two men held, Spider and commissioner of police.

"You saved my life," Kirkpatrick said thickly.

Wentworth glanced above him. There were a half-dozen police at the door with machine guns and revolvers. Others were at the windows. He had saved Kirkpatrick, yes, but he was doomed. What chance to run the gauntlet of that lead? It would drive the glass from his windows in a breath.

"You saved my life," Kirkpatrick said again, more clearly. "It's a shame, Spider, because… you're under arrest." His gun came up slowly.

Wentworth dropped to his knees before Kirkpatrick and his right hand gun slapped the weapon from the other's hand. The commissioner's grip seemed strangely loose. Wentworth's single good arm circled Kirkpatrick's body, heaved him up, and he walked backward to the car a pace or two away. Behind Kirkpatrick his empty gun bore on the police at the head of the steps.

"I won't harm your commissioner," Wentworth called. "But I won't be taken alive!"

Men started down the steps. Wentworth was moving more swiftly now, Kirkpatrick a dead weight in his arms. He seemed to have fainted from the pain of movement, the dragging of his leg. Wentworth staggered with his weight. Impossible to enter his own car this way, with only one arm. He moved swiftly around in front of his car, stumbling, reeling under his burden.

"Get back!" Wentworth shouted fiercely. "I don't want to fire on police, but I won't be taken alive!"

Those leveled guns were blanked out by Kirkpatrick's body. The men hesitated… and Wentworth was behind his own car. Instantly, he eased Kirkpatrick to the running board, sprang into the commissioner's waiting car. The chauffeur was dead behind the wheel, gun in hand. Wentworth thrust him aside, got the car rolling.

"Halt!" he heard the police shouting. "Halt, or we'll fire!"

Wentworth laughed harshly and shoved down the accelerator. If he lived to reach the corner... On the running board of his deserted car, he saw Kirkpatrick's head lift. He couldn't swear to it at this distance, but it seemed to him that Kirkpatrick smiled.

"Shoot at the tires!" Was it Kirkpatrick who cried, that? But it couldn't be. Even for the man who saved his life, there would be no swerving from the stern path of duty for Kirkpatrick. No, it was one of his men... but Kirkpatrick didn't countermand it. His head was sagging again. Unconscious? Then the blast of those many guns ripped the street wide open.

The limousine staggered as if from a hurricane wind. The rear tires went out. Lead pattered like terribly driven hailstones against its body and then, miraculously, he was around the corner. One-handed, Wentworth fought that bucking wheel, made another corner. A taxi was at the curb, its driver huddled in a doorway for protection. When Wentworth reeled to the pavement, he turned and fled, screaming. Terror was in the streets.

Sobbing for breath, Wentworth climbed behind the wheel of the cab. It was labor even to breathe, an incredible task to shift gears and get under way. Under the spur of the gas, the taxi swerved like a drunken man. Still, a smile jerked at the strained corners of Wentworth's mouth. Kirkpatrick was safe. His men had... had not been ungrateful.

THERE WERE blanks in Wentworth's memory of that drive. He knew that he stripped the make-up from his face, that he left the Spider's cape in the cab. He rambled sickeningly as he drove his flagging strength to reach the home of his doctor—a man for whom he had done too many services, and paid too well, for him ever to talk. If he had known that Wentworth was the Spider, perhaps he might have been tempted. But he could not know. Charges of the police, for a friend, were not conviction.

The doctor, himself, opened the door, and Wentworth reeled over the sill and slumped to the floor. He regained consciousness under a blazing white light. The doctor's grim-lined face lifted, came slowly into focus.

"That will hold you for awhile," Dr. Rogers said shortly. "How do you feel?"

"Don't be a fool," Wentworth grumbled at him. "Did you give me an anti-tetanus shot?"

Dr. Rogers nodded. His hair was crisp gray, but it was asprawl on his forehead now. "The shoulder wound was clean. No bones hit, but there's a sprain there, too. You'll be laid up at least a week."

Wentworth laughed harshly, swung his legs off the table and grasped it for support as vertigo swam in his brain. It passed and he straightened, glanced down at his body. He was naked, his thigh and calf studded with strips of court plaster, his body bandaged.

"Not a chance," he said thickly. "Hadn't you heard? There's a war on. My clothes, Doctor. Besides, old man, I can't ask you to risk harboring me. They send men to jail for that, you know."

"You'll land in jail, too, if you try to go out like that," Dr. Rogers said curtly. "Besides… there's nothing you can do."

Wentworth's head jerked up. "Nothing I can do?" he said

queerly. "There's something strange in your voice. What do you mean?"

Dr. Rogers shook his head brusquely. "What I said."

Wentworth peered at him intently and felt the blood drain from his face. He was acutely aware of his surroundings in that moment, of the bright sunlight streaming in through the shaded windows, the smell of antiseptics and Dr. Rogers' weary face.

"What do you mean?" Wentworth demanded sharply. "Is it Kirkpatrick?"

"He's all right—flesh wound in the thigh. On the job, I understand. The newspapers are making quite a fuss over him." Dr. Rogers turned away. "I'll give you a shot, if you've got to go rambling around."

Wentworth took a sharp step forward, seized the doctor by the shoulder. "Give me the newspaper," he said shortly. "And don't try any tricks with that shot. I've got work to do."

Dr. Rogers filled a hypodermic needle, handed Wentworth the newspaper as he came back. Wentworth seized it, scarcely felt the needle slide home in his arm. His eyes quested fiercely over the front page, and a cry tore from his heart. He sank back against the operating table and stared unseeingly before him. The jumbled black type of that front page danced and cavorted before his eyes. One phrase, a dozen words... *"The horribly muti-lated body of a girl identified as Nita van Sloan...."*

Wentworth's head swung from side to side, slowly, without meaning. He whispered a word, a name... His eyes... He felt himself falling, felt the doctor's arms strongly about him. That was all....

CHAPTER 12
THE DOOMED THOUSANDS

THE STRENGTH was gone out of Wentworth's soul. It was his body that fought on in the days that followed. Dr. Rogers' opiates kept him in a dim, half-waking trance. When finally he was allowed to regain full consciousness, he lay apathetic, staring at the ceiling.

"I had to give you that opiate, Wentworth," Dr. Rogers apologized. "If you had gone out in that shape, you would have certainly been killed. As it is, you'll be fully recovered in another week or so."

Wentworth gestured a vague forgiveness. After all, delay could count for little, if Nita… His face quivered with pain. "The story I read in the newspaper…" he said hesitantly.

"True, I'm afraid, poor girl." Dr. Rogers bowed his head. "Commissioner Kirkpatrick was… satisfied of the identity."

Wentworth tried to bring realization to his mind, to his heart. It wasn't possible that Nita—deliberately, he forced the phrase— had been tortured to death. A shock ran over his body. Why, as God was in Heaven, men had done this thing to Nita—and still *lived!* The Spider was on the same earth with them—and they still lived!

Wentworth stiffly flung back the covers, swung his feet to the floor. His face was still and white, awful.

"My clothes, Rogers," he said flatly.

Dr. Rogers stared at him, and obeyed. He was silent while Wentworth clothed himself. Even when Wentworth deliberately checked his two automatics and thrust them home in his holsters, Rogers did not speak.

Wentworth held out his hand formally. "Thank you for your efforts, Doctor Rogers," he said. "If I don't show up again, ample provision is made for you in my will."

Rogers held his hand in both of his. "Be careful, Dick," he said quietly. "I've done what I could to build you up, but you're far from strong. If you exert yourself violently, or suffer some shock—" he snapped his fingers—"you're apt to keel over like that."

Wentworth smiled faintly, "I'll remember, Doctor Rogers." As if anything could shock him now! But he must be careful, he must guard his strength. Nothing must happen to prevent his coming face to face with the Whisper and his torturers! He was glad, soon, to take a taxi, for the perspiration of weakness was on his forehead.

The cab sped southward toward the address he had given, and Wentworth leaned back against the cushions. He was picking up the battle, where he had left off to save Kirkpatrick's life. Not in useless skirmishes with gangsters, but on the trail of the Whisper himself. He was going to call on the sister of the district attorney!

Wentworth had had a passing glimpse of himself in a mirror and did not believe that anyone would recognize this haggard, hollow-eyed man as Richard Wentworth. If anyone did… Wentworth's arm pressed down again his automatic. No one was going to stop him before he exacted his vengeance—no one!

Once on the trip to the old-fashioned mansion on lower

Lexington, in which the district attorney lived, Wentworth stopped the cab for a newspaper. There was a fear in him that he could scarcely overcome, as he lifted the paper, and a cringing in his heart that he knew would be there forever. On such a page as this… He closed his mind on the thought, skimmed the headlines.

"Nineteen police slain by raiders," ran one, and the story said that criminals had now murdered more than three hundred of the city police. From the context, it was plain that, under the Whisper, nightly forays were made against officers. The dragnet had failed. Courts were at a standstill, for witnesses feared to testify in any type of criminal case. Kirkpatrick had refused to ask for National Guard help.

"If my policemen, experienced as they are in fighting criminals, cannot cope with the situation," he said, "what chance would the youngsters of the National Guard have?"

Wentworth nodded in stiff agreement. Kirkpatrick was right, of course, but the crime toll… His eye ran down the columns. Dozens of holdups and five murders, besides the attacks on the police, were chronicled. The city was in panic and there was a movement to displace Kirkpatrick. As if any other man could serve half so well!

Wentworth read these things and knew that New York was tottering toward an anarchical doom. The Whisper should not escape!

The cab drew to a halt before the mansion of the district attorney, and Wentworth walked steadily past the double police guard at the door. If they recognized him… but he was not the same man he had been a week before. His body was gaunt, and there was a droop to his left shoulder because of injuries. The confident, sure stride, that had been his, was gone, and though he did not know it, his head had lost its erectness. It was a pitiful travesty of the Spider that was going forth to battle the most powerful enemy New York had ever known!

ONLY WHEN he lifted the lids that seemed so heavy, when the gray-blue fire of his eyes blazed forth, did Richard Wentworth betray the flame that raged behind that enfeebled husk of a body.

"Mr. Richards to see Miss Louis," Wentworth told the butler. "A matter concerning Mr. Delehanty." It worked.

The butler went away, but it was the quick feet of Phyllis Louis that returned. She came slowly, then, into the reception room where Wentworth stood.

"I don't understand," she said.

"It's soon explained," Wentworth said quietly. "Your brother, Delehanty, was being blackmailed. The mails were used. That is where I come into the case."

Phyllis Louis retreated a step, sank into a chair. "Sit down," she said emptily. "No, I didn't know he had asked the government for help. What did you want to know?"

Wentworth's lips were stiff with the effort at control. This was so slow, so passive, when he longed for violent action, for the blazing guns of vengeance. But this was the path he must tread. He spoke carefully.

"I must know—everything," he said shortly. "Your brother was very sparing in details, but begged us not to approach the district attorney at this point. I do not know of any reason for continued secrecy, however."

Phyllis Louis twisted her hands in her lap. Above her black mourning dress, her face was startlingly white; her eyes seemed very large.

"I will tell you what I know," she said dully. "It's little enough. Several years ago, my brother was out with some friends. There was drinking, an automobile accident. A girl was killed, and they abandoned her body beside the road. Delehanty said it was his fault—to what extent I don't know. He was sure that if it became known, it would force Thomas to prosecute him. You can see what that would do to his career."

Wentworth nodded. He wanted to hurl at her the fact that Delehanty's fears had cost another girl her life—had started the awful train of fire that led to the present conflagration. But the sister could not help it, and he wanted information.

"I see," he said dryly. "The name of the person who was blackmailing him?"

Phyllis shook her head, "I don't know, Mr. Richards."

Wentworth whipped to his feet. The blaze of his eyes made her shrink back in her chair.

"I will stand for no trifling," he said sternly.

"I don't know," Phyllis whispered. "Honestly, I don't."

"Then the names of those who were in the car with him!"

"I can tell you at least one of those," she said slowly, "but they had nothing to do with the blackmailing. I'm sure of that, because...."

"Never mind that," Wentworth said harshly. "The name?"

Phyllis Louis stared at him. She was coming slowly to her feet. "There is something about you," she whispered, "that... You have no right to talk to me this way!"

Wentworth forced himself to calmness. In his frantic desire for information, he was behaving... not quite sanely. "I apologize, Miss Louis," he said slowly. "But you understand that this may hold the key to this entire criminal conspiracy that is shaking New York. Please, now, the name?"

Phyllis hesitated. "Very well. But I'm sure he has nothing to do with it. His name..." She broke off, as a man suddenly appeared outlined in the large French window. He held a snub-nosed automatic. It was another of the Whisper's men, about to close the lips of another member of the Louis family. He was about....

But even as the thug's automatic leveled on the girl's abruptly stupefied face, Wentworth fired. His gun, whipped forth like lightning, beat the other to the shot. There was a scream from that window, a violent threshing... then the gunman pitched off into space.

Wentworth turned, barely in time to see the wild-eyed newcomer striding into the room. "Oh, Martin, I'm glad you've come. This is Mr. Richards, a government man...."

Wentworth faced about reluctantly. Martin Meggs—of all the damnable luck! Perhaps, the one man aside from Kirkpatrick who would recognize him. Even as he saw the start of Meggs' recognition, Wentworth whipped out a gun.

"Not a sound, either of you!"

Meggs took an angry stride forward. Phyllis muffled a scream. "Oh, what is it?" she cried.

"This government man," said Meggs heavily, "is the man who killed your brother, Richard Wentworth! I'm glad you're not dead, as reported, Wentworth. Now I can have the pleasure of killing you!"

Wentworth's lips parted in a thin smile and, before the thrust of his eyes, Meggs dropped back a half-pace. "Miss Louis," he said slowly. "I'm still waiting for the name of the man who blackmailed your brother. I'll give you until I count five, then I'm going to shoot down this man. He is your fiancé, I believe?"

Phyllis stared at him, her eyes stretching wide and wider. Abruptly, she screamed! At the same instant, Meggs leaped to the attack!

Wentworth swore, violently. He could not shoot, of course, and he was no match physically now for Meggs. He faded away from the man's rush, dodged a swift punch and lashed out with the gun. Meggs pitched forward, unconscious, to the rug. Wentworth turned toward the girl, but she had fled screaming into the hall. Police were rushing toward the front door. Wentworth darted after the girl, but she was on her way toward the police, to let them in. He couldn't reach her in time!

WENTWORTH TURNED and fled toward the rear of the building. The butler saw him coming but the gun in his hand sent the man leaping aside. Through a butler's pantry, a kitchen where a woman cook screamed, out the back door. Wentworth's breath came in strained gasps. He was weaker than he would have believed possible.

A chauffeur was running toward the house across the back lawn, a wrench grasped in his hand. Wentworth barked out a laugh. Where there was a chauffeur, there would be a car! He squeezed the trigger and dug a bullet into the earth ahead of the running man. The chauffeur brought to a stiff halt, stared at Wentworth, then turned and fled for the near-by alley gate. Wentworth ran, too, but toward the garage. When he swung in behind the steering wheel of the big limousine, he was trembling with weakness. But he could not pause. He kicked the starter, slammed into gear and sent the limousine hurtling backward along the driveway. He was lucky in one thing. The police had gone into the building and there was no one to block his escape.

One thing was clear. He could not again depend upon running for escape. He must have a car nearby, always, for flight. He tooled the big car across town until he was near one of the garages which, scattered about the city, housed machines for the Spider's use. Quickly, he made the transfer—and turned back toward Louis' mansion! His task was doubly difficult now, but he could not abandon it for that reason. He was more than ever convinced that if he could wring the truth from Phyllis, he would have a clue that would lead to the Whisper! Somehow, it must be accomplished—and at once.

Wentworth was within a block of the Louis mansion, slowing his car to a halt, when he saw Phyllis and Martin Meggs hurrying down the short walk to the street. A car was waiting for them there, but, even as the door swung open for them, another sedan whirled around the corner and pinned the waiting machine to the curb. A half-dozen men poured from its open doors. Meggs yanked out a gun, squeezed off a single shot. There was an answering hail of lead. One of the police on guard at the door was hurled against the glass panel, pitched backward through the shattered pane. Meggs collapsed to the pavement. Phyllis was hurled bodily into the gangster car and it rolled swiftly on again!

What now?

The whole thing had taken only a few seconds. Wentworth slammed into gear and took the trail! He was a half-block behind, when the machine ahead turned the corner and, mechanically, he noted that the number on the license plate was low—*I-ZZ-40*. He took the corner in a wide, skidding turn—and the machine had vanished! It must have tremendous acceleration to be able to reach the next corner so swiftly. Wentworth pumped gas to his own powerful motor and flashed toward the turn, went skating into it—narrowly missed a speeding taxi. Still no sight of the fleeing car!

He must find it.

With mounting alarm, Wentworth circled two blocks in a frenzy of search—in vain. He raced back toward the scene of the kidnaping. Damn it, there was some trickery here! There must be some hidden alley, some garage… He jammed on brakes as he spotted a narrow garage squeezed in between two buildings. He ran toward the doors, gun in hand, peered into the dark interior. Empty! He stared down at the pavement. There were dark, smeared stains where tires had been skidded in a furious curve. People did not drive into garages that way, ordinarily. This garage had been used all right. The car had slammed into this hiding place, and the moment pursuit had dashed past, had emerged to take up some other line of flight!

WENTWORTH SPRANG back to the car... but he had no chance now of locating the fleeing car himself. He would have to call on the police. Once Phyllis was found and released, he could once more try for information. Delay, *delay!* He was afire with impatience. He whirled his car, glimpsed Meggs being lifted into an ambulance before the Louis home. He parked near a drugstore and hurried into a telephone booth, shot through a call to Kirkpatrick.

Kirkpatrick's voice was curt, hurried as he answered. "Wentworth speaking," Wentworth threw out words. "Phyllis Louis was just kidnaped. The license number of the snatch car is I-ZZ-forty."

Kirkpatrick repeated the number, hurled an order at someone near. "Wait, Dick," he said. "You must wait. That license number...."

Impatiently, Wentworth repeated it.

"You can't be mistaken?" Kirkpatrick asked slowly. "I can't understand that. That is the license number of... District Attorney Louis!"

In a curiously strained voice, Wentworth answered, "You're not making a mistake, Kirk? But, of course, you aren't! Good Lord, Kirk, can't you see? I went to the Louis home to demand from Phyllis the name of the man who was blackmailing her brother. A short while afterward, she is kidnaped. In other words, the need to kidnap her didn't arise until I had asked that question. It must be a fake all along. Louis is the guilty man."

"You're crazy," Kirkpatrick snapped. "Look here, Dick. I want you to surrender here within the next hour!"

"I may be crazy," Wentworth said slowly, "but it's a fact that Louis got his first publicity out of his friendship for the Chinatown tongs. He made peace between two warring factions, you remember? And the Whisper's men are Chinese!"

"Will you surrender?" Kirkpatrick demanded again.

Wentworth said slowly, "Wait a minute, Kirk. Maybe I will. Just give me time to think something through. I'll call you back within fifteen minutes."

Hurriedly, Wentworth hung up on Kirkpatrick's call and ran to his car, got away from the vicinity, fast.

It was almost a half-hour before Wentworth called Kirkpatrick again.

"All right, Kirk," he said swiftly. "I'll surrender in three hours' time, at your office. But you must do certain things for me or the deal is off. I can prove my innocence by that time, but I want District Attorney Louis told right away that he must be there in three hours' time. I want Meggs, too. He's a witness to what Phyllis Louis said. I'd like to have Phyllis, instead, but that may not be possible. Louis can arrange for him to be there. He only suffered a scalp wound and is ready to leave the hospital." He took a breath.

"I will also prove at that time that Delehanty Louis did give out the information about Ada Hamilton which caused her death. I know the person he told—and the name of the Whisper!"

"Give it to me!" Kirkpatrick ordered violently. "I'll bring him in, if it's the last thing I ever do!"

Wentworth laughed shortly. "Maybe you will—if the Whisper lives that long! You can tell Louis this, too. I know where the prisoners of the Whisper are kept and they will be among my witnesses. Without them you'd never get a conviction. And I'll surrender in three hours, Kirk—if I'm still alive at that time!"

He slammed up the receiver on Kirkpatrick's cry, and ran from the booth. It would be dark within an hour and he still had a few preparations to make. He saw to his guns and, once more, he donned the disguise of the Spider—it might be for the last time!

CHAPTER 13
LAIR OF THE WHISPER

WENTWORTH HAD lied to Kirkpatrick about nothing except his hopes of proving his own innocence, and that did not matter greatly. He had promised that only death would prevent his keeping the appointment to surrender, but he thought that death would be obliging. The Spider was going to invade the Whisper's lair, single-handed, intent only on killing the Whisper.

Wentworth pulled his car to a halt in the alley that abutted the rear of District Attorney Louis' home, strode openly into the grounds. Here, he was convinced, he would find the lair of the Whisper.

There was a policeman on guard at the kitchen door, Wentworth saw at once. The Spider stalked straight forward as if he had not spotted the man. His cape was drawn close about him like a coat, and the crouching hunch to his shoulders, that was characteristic of the Spider, he had not yet assumed. When he was twenty feet from the porch where the policeman stood, Wentworth gave a violent start, turned and darted toward the corner of the house. Now the cape flaunted from his shoulders and here, for any man to see, was the Spider himself!

The policeman uttered a loud cry. "The Spider! The Spider!" Wentworth saw him fumbling for his gun, but distances had been calculated to a nicety. He reached the corner of the house an instant before the man's gun crashed! Close against the wall, the Spider crouched while the pounding feet of the policeman raced toward him. His out-thrust foot caught the man's ankle, sprawled him headlong. The gun flew in a glittering arc from his hand, and Wentworth flung himself back toward the porch. The heavy thrust of his heel shattered the lock, and he was inside the house. Two servants fled, shrieking, from his path.

Even from that brief exertion, Wentworth was panting heavily, but he was close to safety. The mansion was an historic landmark in New York, and it had not been difficult to find floor-plans. He knew where he was going. Two strides took him to the basement door. He whipped it open, darted down. A small flashlight played ahead of him, found the heating-plant, and a brief smile touched his lips. As he had figured, from the plans, the furnace was huge. Long bounds took him to its door. He eased it open, soundlessly, seized hold of a projection and slid feet first into the fire-box. It was just possible to twist about inside, silently close the door. It was harder to still his violent breathing, but he managed it before the lights blazed on in the basement and policemen came creeping down the stairs.

This much, Wentworth had planned beforehand—the rest was up to the Whisper. Police headquarters would hear shortly that the Spider had dashed into the basement of Louis' home, and vanished! It was quite obvious that the Whisper had a pipeline into headquarters, so he would shortly know that fact, too. To him, it could have only one meaning—if Wentworth's deductions as to his lair were correct. The Spider had penetrated his secret and had vanished into that hiding place! Before long, then, he could hope that the Whisper's searching men would come seeking him, and reveal that secret entrance!

Rapidly, the police canvassed the basement and their shouts told him they found all windows and doors locked from the inside. They stood, four men in police blue, huddled at the foot of the steps.

"Damn it, the butler saw him come down here!"

"Well, he ain't here... look, we better call headquarters right now!"

In a breath, they were all clattering noisily up the steps. The door clapped shut... but the light stayed on. They would be standing guard outside that closed door. Now, he need only wait. Wentworth settled himself as comfortably as possible. It was a big gamble he had made, but he had to be right. He had to be! Somewhere below this building, in the ancient, abandoned subway drift that old street plans showed, was the Whisper's lair. It had been walled off solid years ago, forgotten. Beneath this building... Wentworth's breath caught in his throat. It was strange that he stood not in a fire-box, or on an oil burner but on the floor of the basement itself. Of course, oil burners were removable... but that furnace door had been easy to open quietly. WITH MOUNTING excitement, Wentworth squeezed on his flashlight and examined the hinges. Freshly oiled! His hand showed in the light and there was no dust upon his collodion-tipped fingers, none on his clothing. And that was a strange thing in a furnace which had not been burning for a month or more. Almost furtively, Wentworth put the light of his flash upon the floor beneath his feet. It seemed to be a solid sheet of concrete. He dared not test it for hollowness lest the sound of his blows reverberate below him... if he were right. Feverishly, he searched the sides of the furnace for some hidden catch....

There was nothing he could find except the projections, part of the original casting, on which the gratings formerly had rested. He crouched to examine them, and his lips drew taut against his teeth. Castings were made all in one piece. This support showed a distinct groove all around, separating it from the body of the fire-box. It was pure deduction of course, but Wentworth knew instinctively that he was right. He had found the entrance to the Whisper's lair.

It meant he dared not wait for word to reach the Whisper, for him to send men seeking the Spider! There was no other hiding place than this furnace and presently the police would hit upon it.

Deliberately, Wentworth grasped the support and tried it sideways, up, down, turning—and it came loose in his hands!

Inside the narrow opening from which it had come was an iron ring whose metal showed no slightest trace of rust. Wentworth drew a gun, crouched motionless for a moment. His heart was pounding, furiously. He had no means of knowing what lay below this furnace floor. He might descend amid the Whisper's men.

Wentworth's lips twisted. Police would come seeking, presently. He ripped off the cape, shed his coat and drew his cape back on his shoulders. He wadded his coat against the furnace door, and from his pocket lighter, spilled a few drops of its inflammable fluid upon the fabric. He touched flame to it, watched the cloth begin to smolder. Then, with steady hand, he pulled the secret ring!

For a full half-minute nothing happened. Smoke grew dense in the enclosed space where he crouched. He muffled his face in his cape and then, slowly, with utmost steadiness, the floor moved downward beneath him like an elevator floor. Below him was absolute darkness. Cautiously, Wentworth pinched out a thread of light from his hand-shielded flashlight, saw the oval mouth of a tunnel coming into sight. An instant later, he whisked through that and, with the same slow steadiness, the furnace floor started upward again.

Raw earth was over and around him, supported by fresh-cut timbers. Wentworth hefted his guns and crept forward. Thirty, forty feet, the corridor ran in a straight line. There was an abrupt right-angle turn and, before him, he saw a dim shadow of light. He flicked off his own flash and emerged presently on a narrow gallery against the arched concrete and brick wall of the old subway drift. That he was prepared for, but the sight that met his eyes below raised a shout of fury to his lips that he barely pressed down. Lining the walls, scattered about the floor were a hundred ancient and cruel devices of torture. A man was stretched terribly, upon a rack, shoulders wrenched to the breaking-point by those merciless spiked drums. A girl swung by her thumbs in a torture scaffold, but worse than either of these was... the treadmill!

ITS SIDES were smooth, without any hold at all and at its lower end was a pit that blazed with incredible, white-hot heat. Two girls were imprisoned in that shaft, with freedom always mockingly before them, if only the moving treadmill under their feet would remain motionless for a moment. They struggled to reach its top, but the faster they strove to walk, to run, the faster the treadmill moved under their feet. When exhaustion claimed them, they would fall into that terrible pit....

He could not see the faces of the girls. The strong light behind them was blinding, but there was something terribly familiar— hauntingly dear—about that second girl, the one who struggled nearest to the blazing pit. Wentworth shook his head, dragged a hand across his eyes. It couldn't be... His anxiety, his hopes were playing him fiendish tricks. He peered again, leaning forward from the gallery He forgot everything—the men in their purple robes and devil masks that moved about their torture machines, the tunnel behind him and the light that blazed from the pit. It couldn't be... *Good God, it was!*

The girl's face swung toward him, and he heard her voice lifted in a sudden, sharp cry, "Dick! *Dick, behind you!*"

Wentworth tried to whirl but there was lead in his limbs. A fleeting remembrance of the doctor's warning struck him. "Any sudden shock, and you're apt to keel over…" Shock! But this was joy! Nita, Nita was alive! Perhaps doomed on that torture belt, unless he could save her, but alive, and….

Wentworth tried to turn. His guns weighed a ton in each hand, and there was a devil-masked man on the gallery just behind him. One of Wentworth's guns blasted, but without direction. He felt himself falling even before the blow the Whisper's man aimed at his head crashed home on his skull.

CHAPTER 14
HELL'S TREADMILL

IT WAS Nita's voice in his ear that brought him back to consciousness. Not the soft and lovely accents he remembered, but strained and frantic, pleading with him. "Dick!" she gasped. "Dick, in heaven's name. I… I can't keep it up much longer!"

Wentworth fought for recovery, felt his feet moving in a numb walking, stiffness and life crept through his body.

"Oh, thank heavens," Nita sobbed… then her voice went *away* from him!

Abruptly, Wentworth realized what was happening. He was on the treadmill. Nita had been supporting him, and now… her voice was going away from him! Wentworth turned dizzily, his eyes still barely able to focus, saw Nita huddled upon the moving belt of the treadmill—moving toward the fiery pit. With a bound, he reached her, snatched her to her feet. The brink was only short inches away now. He caught her into his arms, began to toil against that moving belt.

There were other forms ahead of him—seven girls and a single man—all walking, *walking* away from death. They dared not move more rapidly lest exhaustion come too soon. Always behind him was the pit. Wentworth could feel its heat strike like a hammer against his back.

But Nita's dear form was in his arms, her face resting close to his. She was half-conscious from exhaustion, her own long labors on the treadmill and that last sharp struggle to keep him from falling to his death.

What fiendish purpose had the Whisper served by killing someone else, clothing her in Nita's garments so that she would be identified as his love? But Wentworth knew, even as he asked the question. He had tortured Wentworth almost to the point of robbing him of all desire to live, and he had kept Nita alive as a hostage if the Spider ever should penetrate his defenses. She was in his arms now... but how long would they both survive? Even if he escaped this treadmill, he had given his promise to Kirkpatrick to surrender. He would keep that promise—if he lived.

Wentworth's eyes glanced fiercely about him and Nita stirred, fought to get on her feet. Wentworth's arms tightened about her, but he was forced to set her down. His strength was equal to no more. She took up the burden of the endless walking—walking away from death.

"Why did you come here, Dick?" she whispered. "What have they done to you? Your face...."

Wentworth remembered the gaunt-lined face that was his now.

Sibilant, mocking laughter struck upon his ears, seemed to fill all that vast chamber, and Wentworth's eyes swung about to behold the Whisper himself! No doubt about that tall, taunting figure on the gallery—*on the gallery!* Good God! Then he had come down through the furnace... the clue of the smoldering coat which Wentworth had left to lead the police had been blotted out!

"No, no, Spider," came the whispering voice. "I'm afraid you won't get out."

WENTWORTH SWORE in his despair and the Whisper came slowly down from the gallery and stood, not more than two yards from the reach of Wentworth's hands—but as hopelessly beyond reach as if the width of the earth separated them! His hand touched a long lever.

"You're tired of that slow walking, aren't you, Wentworth? We'll see if we can't remedy that!"

The lever moved a notch and the speed of the treadmill increased. Ahead of Wentworth, the man cried out brokenly. He stumbled, fell, and the belt dragged him back toward the pit. A woman behind him screamed, tried to hurdle his body, fell, struggled up again ahead of him. Nita reached ahead to bring the man to his feet and Wentworth helped her.

"Courage, man!" Wentworth whispered to him. "Help is coming!"

The man peered up into his face. "Help?" His lips formed the word without the strength to speak. Wentworth nodded encouragingly, and, once more, the man took up the struggle, the walking....

Nita's face swung toward Wentworth. She had caught that whispered word, but his lips twisted in denial. She nodded her understanding, but there was a mere weary droop to her shoulders as she fought on against that tireless, fiendish belt. Wentworth's heart stabbed him. Did he have the right to encourage this man to keep at a hopeless struggle?

"Take off your coat," he called.

As he spoke, he whipped off his cape—which the torturers had left upon him to add to his burdens. He was on the point of hurling it toward the Whisper in futile fury when a thought occurred to him. The man's coat was moving toward him on the belt. He caught it with his foot and kicked it ahead of him, did that again while he fought swiftly for clarity. Was it possible to jam the belt with clothing?

He had seen string, wrapped again and again around an axle, jam an electric motor. Grass could so bunch as to stall a lawn mower... Then why not clothing here? He peered down at the narrow slit between the belt and the smooth sides.

Once more, he kicked the coat ahead and then he shouted fiercely, with a note of madness, and began to sprint up the belt, shoving the man and girls from his path.

"Don't, Dick!" Nita cried. "Don't! It will only go faster!"

Even as she spoke, the belt picked up momentum, but Wentworth appeared to have gone mad. He reached a point two-thirds up the belt. He was cursing, screaming. Then he tripped and fell—fell with cape and coat ready in his hands!

Behind them was the fiery pit—ahead was constant toil of the treadmill.

Furiously, he drove them down into the narrow slit on one side of the belt.

The treadway was flexible—it had to be to run over the rollers at top and bottom. It gave a little, and Wentworth fed in the garments. The steel side ground against the back of his hand, rasped the flesh. His hand was in the vise of tread and side, but, despite excruciating pain, it held him motionless for a little—for the instants it took to stuff the garments home.

Then he was moving down the belt again. He struggled to his feet beside Nita and, when he rose, she saw the calmness of his face, glanced at the clothing, and understood. But it would not do for the Whisper to realize what he had planned. Wentworth shook a fist furiously.

"You've got me!" he shouted. "We'll die, all of us, but you won't escape. I told the police who you were!"

The Whisper took a long stride forward. "You couldn't!"

Wentworth laughed aloud. "I did! Listen, I found this lair of yours, didn't I? That should prove it to you! I knew it was somewhere around District Attorney Louis' house. His car was used to kidnap his own sister! It dodged into a garage just around the corner from his house! It was only a few minutes after Wentworth questioned Phyllis that she was kidnaped. Why hadn't it been done before? Because the Whisper hadn't realized the need of it!"

Beneath Wentworth's feet, he felt the belt of the treadmill catch, hesitate, grind on, and fresh hope sprang into his heart.

"If we could get off this belt," Wentworth cried, "we would tear you to pieces with our own hands!"

Heads turned toward him among the tortured ones on the belt. Nita had gained a few inches, when the belt checked. She took longer strides and gained a few more. She had caught Wentworth's meaning. She was to prepare the others for the stopping of the belt. It checked again under their feet.

Wentworth leaned toward the Whisper, shouting furiously to distract his attention. "I know why you did all those things, Whisper! A plain trail, isn't it, pointing to District Attorney Louis! A plain trail... but *a false scent!*"

The Whisper flinched at those words. Wentworth saw his hands fumbling under his robe and knew that he reached for a gun. Wentworth laughed aloud, lifted his voice to drown out the grinding of the treadmill rollers. His plan was working... *working*. If only he could gain a few more moments!

"Yes, a false scent!" he shouted. "Delehanty Louis said, before he died, that he had been blackmailed into telling about Ada Hamilton. Phyllis told me what he was blackmailed about— that accident a long time ago when a girl was killed by his fault. But no one knew of that accident—no one but his friends! The people he thought were his friends, those who were in that accident with her. You were in that accident, Whisper. You were his friend, his *closest* friend—so close, you swore to avenge his death! Whisper, I know you. You are... *Martin Meggs!*"

WITH AN inarticulate cry, that was confession in itself, the Whisper snatched out his gun—and in that instant, the belt ground to a halt! Wentworth dropped to his knees, as the gun crashed and lead whined past within inches of his head, above the side of the treadmill's smooth walls. Ahead of him, girls screamed and he heard Nita cry out.

"Tear him to pieces! He is the one who has tortured us!"

He heard the Whisper's mounting cry, still whispered, terrible in the impotence of its sound. Wentworth jumped high, reached the edge of the treadmill slot and drew himself upward. Power flowed into his muscles, and he flung himself clear. Three girls were grappling with the Whisper. Nita caught up a heavy chain and swung it fiercely—not at his head, but prudently at his unguarded legs! The Whisper yelped and went down.

The Whisper's men were rushing forward now. One of them had a cross-bow. Wentworth snatched up the Whisper's dropped gun and his shot smashed home in the man's throat drove him back against the wall. The cross-bow flew high and, whirling in the air, discharged itself. Wentworth saw the flash of its missile, sailing wide, heard it strike the wall... and splinter into glittering bits of glass! So that secret was out—a disk of glass, sharpened to a razor edge that gashed like a knife under the powerful drive of the cross-bow... and splintered when its fearful work was done to leave no trace of the missile.

Furious women were stamping on the Whisper's body with their high heels. One of them had wrenched off his steel casque, and beneath it, as Wentworth had known, was the terrified, tortured face of Martin Meggs. One of his legs was doubled hideously beneath him, broken by the swipe of Nita's chain. Wentworth could have killed him then, easily. But coolly, he turned his back and took up his guard post with the automatic in his hand. Five more of the Whisper's men, and there were five bullets in the heavy automatic in his hand.

The cavern filled with the heavy beat of the automatic, the high whine of the crossbows' missiles, but one by one the men went down. Behind Wentworth, Meggs' shouts of pain changed to whining pleas of mercy. Nita was beside Wentworth.

"They're torturing him terribly, Dick."

Wentworth laughed fiercely. "I have no bullets to spare!" he said shortly.

Nita's hand closed on his arm. "Please, Dick!"

Wentworth whirled reluctantly, gun lifted. He was too late. The man who had been on the treadmill held the chain Nita had discarded. Even as Wentworth turned, that chain swished down terribly. Meggs saw it coming and screamed. The shriek lifted high, thin, terrible—and the chain lashed home, across his face! Meggs' body jerked convulsively, and there was no movement at all. A last man of the Whisper's gang was rushing up the steps toward the gallery.

Wentworth saw the cross-bow leveled and the gun in his hand spat thunderously. The man was tossed off into space. His arms and legs sprawled wide. He fell, face down, at the foot of the steps—and still Wentworth could hear cries. They seemed to issue from the mouth of the tunnel from which he, himself, had first come. Cries, there! More men of the Whisper—or the police? Either spelled disaster for him. He listened acutely and caught the crisp, clear tones of a voice he knew so well—Commissioner Kirkpatrick.

"Forward men! Don't let one of them escape alive!"

Wentworth's gun sagged. He might as well surrender here, and now there would be no denying that he and the Spider were one—for he wore the Spider's disguise. It had been his hand that had led them here, for the Whisper had not been able to destroy all the evidence that led to this underground tunnel. The smell of scorched cloth was persistent; it would have been strongest in the cold furnace, and Kirkpatrick had a mind as clear as his own for reading clues.

WENTWORTH STARED about him. Was there no way out? Abruptly, a smile touched his lips. Richard Wentworth might still escape—if the Spider died here! With a long bound, he was beside the Whisper's body. He printed the seal of the Spider on his forehead. As he turned away, he caught up the devil-mask. Inside it, as he expected, he found a microphone amplifier. This, then, was the way in which the Whisper had waxed so enormous.

"Stay here, Nita," he whispered. "The Spider is going to die— but remember, the Spider is not Richard Wentworth!"

He sprinted into the darkness, and Nita waited for the arrival of the police. Blue-coated men rushed out and, an instant later, Kirkpatrick swung into view on crutches.

"Thank God, you've come!" Nita cried to Kirkpatrick. "The Spider was here. He killed some men and chased one off into the darkness somewhere."

Kirkpatrick peered down at the Whisper's dead men below, and laughed shortly. "It's easy to see the Spider has been here!" he said. "But where is he now?"

And now a sibilant whisper cut across the tunnel—the voice of the Whisper.

"Here's the Spider!" he cried, and his accent was the sing-song accent of the East. "He killed my master! I kill him!"

On the far side of that fiery pit, washed by the fierce heat from it, stood a figure in the purple robe, the devil-mask of one of the Whisper's men! He held the body of a man, clad in ordinary clothing, high above his head, and, as he finished speaking, he hurled the body into the fiery pit.

"The Spider," he whispered, "is dead!"

On the instant, he whirled and fled into the darkness away from the glare of the pit. Bullets whined after him, but they had no eyes to find him in blackness. As the figure ran, he stripped off purple robe and devil-mask, and there was laughter on Wentworth's lips. It would be easy to find one of the other exits from the inside of the tunnel.

And, with the Spider killed before Kirkpatrick's very eyes, Richard Wentworth could afford to surrender. He glanced at the radio-dial of his watch as he ran. He would be on time, to the dot!